Hang Angel

FREDERICK H. CHRISTIAN

SPHERE BOOKS LIMITED
30/32 Gray's Inn Road, London WC1X 8JL

First published in Great Britain by Sphere Books Ltd 1975

Set in Monotype Baskerville

Printed in Great Britain by
Hazell Watson & Viney Ltd
Aylesbury, Bucks

ISBN 0 7221 6416 5

Another one for Snoopy

A NOTE TO THE READER

In Record Group 60 of the National Archives in Washington DC there is abundant documentary evidence to the effect that for a number of years the United States Department of Justice employed a Special Investigator named Frank Angel, who was directly responsible to the Attorney-General of the United States. There is no record that the events portrayed in this book took place, or that Frank Angel took part in them. Equally, there is no record that he did not.

CHAPTER ONE

Joe Fischer was a handsome sort of a fellow.

This was his own opinion, of course. A disinterested spectator might have pointed out that for all the boy's good features, skin tanned and smooth, body slim and wiry, hands supple and long-fingered, eyes clear and healthy, there was something weak about the set of the mouth, something shifty about the way the eyes returned your glance, something not quite square. Maybe it was just pride. Joe Fischer was as full of pride as a bull is full of wind at corn time.

Right now, he had it in mind to do a little courtin', and he was duded up appropriately. A new blue shirt; Levi pants which, if not new, were at least clean; boots shined and spurs a-jingling, Joe Fischer rode across the prairie tall in the saddle, admiring the shadow his passing figure threw on the ground, thinking how pleased Susie Webb would be to see him.

He'd taken the mountain pass road that morning, the one that curved up into the lower foothills of the Arabelas to the east of the Fischer ranch and then made a wide loop south, crossing the Rio Abajo on its way to join the main Las Vegas road. The Webb ranch was in a shaded stand of timber alongside the river; he could see the place as he came down the long crest of the hill. One of these days he'd marry the Webb girl and take over running it. Kick her snotnosed brother out for a start. It would open the whole range to Fischer stock, which would make Ed happy too. Joe Fischer grinned. That wasn't the reason he fancied being married to Susie Webb.

He stopped at the edge of a trickling creek that joined the Rio Abajo, slicking down his long black hair with water, blowing into a cupped hand to make sure his breath was sweet. Then he swung back aboard the paint, reining sharply back to bring the animal's head up as he cantered up the slope towards the house, a long rising cloud of dust marking his passage.

As he hitched the paint to the rail in front of the porch, the Mexican woman who acted as a housekeeper for the Webbs came around the side of the house, a wicker basket full of half-dried laundry beneath her arm. If she was pleased to see Joe Fischer, her face didn't show it.

'Howdy, there, Deluvina,' Fischer said, smiling ingratiatingly. 'Miss Susie about the place?'

Deluvina nodded, her dark eyes unfriendly and watchful.

'She in the house?'

Again the unfriendly movement of the head. Damn the bitch! Pumped full of that stiff-necked greaser haughtiness. Her son was the same: acted like he figured he was as good as a white man.

'I'll go say hello,' Fischer said. 'You get on with what you're doin', no need to disturb you.'

'*Si, señor*,' Deluvina said, bowing her head. She left on cat feet and Joe Fischer cursed at the feeling she had managed to impart: of having permitted him to go inside. Permitted him, Joe Fischer, to do something! He pushed open the door and called Susie Webb's name. She came to the doorway of the big room at the far end of the corridor, her fresh young face bright with an anticipation that faded to suspicion when she saw who her visitor was.

'Oh, hello, Joe,' she said. 'What do you want?'

The way she said it made Joe Fischer angry. It wasn't the kind of welcome he'd been imagining all the way across the mountains, nothing like. The fact that Susie Webb cordially disliked him had never occurred to Joe. He put her coolness down to woman's wiles: just her way of leading him on, seeing if he had the fire to melt the iceberg. Well, he did, he assured himself.

'Just thought I'd ride over to see you, Susie,' Joe said, pushing the door closed. 'How've you been?'

'Pretty well,' Susie said. 'Joe, I was just getting ready to go out.'

'Aw, no need to dash off, is there. I was figgerin' on settin' an' talkin' awhile.'

'No, I promised to meet Dick, bring his lunch up to the north past—' Something in Joe Fischer's eyes made her pause just for a fleeting moment. No, she told herself. 'Pasture,' she repeated.

'He's working that far out?' Joe asked, artlessly.

'Yes,' Susie said briskly, 'so you see I've—'

She made to walk by him in the narrow corridor but he put his palm flat against the wall, his arm effectively barring her way.

'Oh, Joe, stop that,' she said, pushing ineffectually at his arm. It was a harmless moment. But she was too close, and much too pretty. Her blue eyes sparked with impatience, and she turned, pushing against Joe's chest with both hands. He caught her arms in his hands, pulling her against him. She smelled of soap. Like fresh-cut grass, he thought, bending his head down to kiss her, pinioning the girl against him.

'Joe,' she panted. 'You stop this now. Get away from me.'

'Aw,' he said, his head pursuing her dodging lips. 'Just one li'l ol' kiss, Susie. Come on, you ain't foolin' me none. You know you want it.'

'Joe,' the girl said. Something in her voice stopped him for a second and he stared at her, surprised.

'Joe,' she repeated. 'Let go of me or I'll scream.'

'Now I know you're givin' me the runaround,' he grinned. 'Ain't nobody gonna come if you scream.' He pulled her tight, wrapping his arms around her, thrusting himself against her. And she screamed, screamed, screamed until Joe managed to get a hand across her mouth, stifling the shocking noise, his eyes bugging with astonishment at her treachery. 'What you want to do that for?' he said. 'What in the hell you want to do that for?'

He took his hand away and the girl screamed again, and without even thinking Joe hit her with the flat of his hand. Susie Webb went back on her heels, tears of shock in her eyes. She banged against the wall, spinning, and sat down on the floor as the door burst open and Deluvina's fifteen-year-old son Pedro ran in, a pistol in his hand. Joe Fischer still wasn't thinking properly, but he saw the gun and he reacted instantaneously. His hand flickered down towards the holstered sixgun at his side, faster than the eye could follow. The heavy boom of the weapon in the confined space of the hallway was like the sound of a cannon, and the slug took the kid right below the sternum, blowing his heart apart, picking up the slight body as if it had been a rag doll and hurling it in a tattered heap ten yards outside the open door. Joe Fischer stood, his mouth open, the gun smoking in his hand, only just becoming aware of the enormity of what he had done. He didn't even hear Susie Webb come up off the floor, pure blinded rage propelling her, landing like a demented hellcat on Joe Fischer's back, her hands clawed like talons, raking his skin. As her nails dug into him, Fischer reacted with a bellowing roar, shaking Susie off his back as if she had been a small child. She sprawled to one side as he whirled on her; then she went for his face again, desperation in her eyes, the breath whistling through her lips. Her bright blonde hair had come unfastened from the ribbon which tied it back and it swung long and loose.

'Stop it!' Fischer shouted, grabbing at her, keeping his face averted so that she could not reach him with her nails. He felt, rather than saw her knee coming up, and then the sharp pain of the wicked rising blow into the groin hit him with a numbing shock. The rage in his eyes now made the girl fall back in terror and Joe came after her, grabbing for her shoulder, nothing in his mind except the intention to punish, to hurt, to act. The flimsy cotton blouse tore as the girl pulled away, trying for the door of the bedroom behind her. It ripped from collar to waist and Susie instinctively clasped her hands over herself to cover her nakedness. Joe Fischer tore her hands away with a rough gesture, feasting his eyes on her lissome body. He pinned her against the wall with his left hand, pawing her with the other. The girl stood stock-still, her eyes wide and terrified like some forest creature trapped by a merciless predator.

'Joe,' she managed. 'No, Joe. Don't do this. Don't do this, Joe.'

He started to fumble with his pants and she screamed again, bucking against him, making enough room to move, to try to get to the door. Now Joe Fischer growled with anger and hit the girl, his clenched fist catching her at the nape of the neck. She fell to the floor, on her knees, head hanging, long hair flowing like a golden waterfall to the boardsrough. Sobbing, she tried to writhe away from the reaching hands, but Fischer dragged her to her feet. This time he ripped the rest of her blouse away and lurched against her. His hands tugged at her skirt, and then under it. She screamed, the last despairing sound of a drowning soul. Then Fischer hit her again, and her knees buckled. There was a roaring in her head, and her eyes would not focus. And then he was on her.

CHAPTER TWO

He wasn't much more than a kid, but he had a gun. That made him a man, for all that he looked no more than twenty. Fresh-faced, clear-eyed, dressed in faded denim pants and a blue work shirt, his boots scuffed and worn, there wasn't anything about him to set him apart from any dozen kids you'd see in any dozen towns like this one except for the one thing: that huge Navy Colt held in his right hand.

'Fischer!' he yelled. His voice was tight with held anger. He stood, legs spraddled, in the middle of the dusty single street of the Crossing, thumb curled over the spur of the pistol hammer, the 7″ barrel pointing just upwards of the horizontal: the personification of a man spoiling for a fight. Which, agreed the few onlookers who'd seen him boil into town scattering panicked chickens and somnolent noonday dogs, was just about exactly what he was. So they had sought flimsy shelter behind the corners of buildings, inside windows around whose edges they now peered, or doorways from whose depths they squinted, careful not to expose any portion of their own bodies. Meanwhile the kid out in the flat yellow shadowless sunshine stood glaring at the doorway of the saloon as if it were a living thing, so treacherous its every movement must be watched.

'Fischer!' he yelled again. 'Come out here and crawl, you sonofabitch!'

Silence. You couldn't hear the sharply indrawn breaths of every man in town who heard the challenge. No one had ever used that kind of talk with one of the Fischers.

'Fischer!' the boy shouted. 'Do I have to come in and *drag* you out?'

Still not a sound. The watchers up and down the street waited breathlessly for the next development. If the kid was aware of the eyes riveted upon him, he gave no sign of it. He stood there in the street waiting, as if watching some clock that only he could see.

Almost as if he'd counted ten to himself, he nodded. He stuck the Navy Colt into a dog-eared Army flap-holster cut away to expose the triggerguard and hammer, and then stepped up on to the porch of Luskum's Silver King and pushed through the batwings and went inside. Before the doors had quit swinging, the men who had been watching from the safety of nearby doorways scurried across the empty street to find a better vantage point by one of the windows of the Silver King, or near the doorposts of the batwings through which the kid had just entered the place. There wasn't a man in the town wasn't anxious to see what the outcome of the kid's reckless challenge would be. This was Big Ed Fischer's town. It operated under Fischer's rule, according to Fischer law. Anyone challenging that rule or those laws had better be ready to die for his beliefs.

'Ain't that young Dick Webb?' muttered one grizzled oldster, shoving and poking as he tried to get enough of a sight of the goings-on to have something to talk about afterwards.

'Sure is, Dad,' said the man standing in front of him. 'See for yourself.'

The old-timer scuttled into the space the taller man had made, peering into the gloomy interior of the Silver King.

'So 'tis,' whispered the old man in surprise. 'What in the hell's bitin' him?'

'Search me, Dad,' said the big man. 'But whatever it is, he sure as hell looks about ready to bite back!'

He wasn't exaggerating. Dick Webb was standing in the centre of the long room, which had about a dozen men in it. He had eyes for only one: Joe Fischer.

Fischer looked as if he'd have given a sack of money to be anyplace but where he was. His eyes wouldn't meet those of the boy; instead they flickered restlessly from face to face, as if seeking assistance. But nobody moved. Nobody showed any kind of expression at all. The look on Dick Webb's face wasn't the kind that made a man think butting in on his scrap would make sense. Anyway, nobody was too averse to the possibility of seeing one of the high-and-mighty

Fischers taken down a couple of notches. As long as they weren't seen to be associated with whoever did it. So they stayed perfectly still in their seats, ready to hit the floor if and when the shooting started. Stray bullets killed a man just as dead as carefully-aimed ones.

'Webb,' Fischer said, raising his hands away from his sides. 'I ain't goin' to fight with you.' His voice was careful, edged with fear, the voice of a man afraid to precipitate the wrath of the gods.

'By God you are!' gritted Dick Webb. 'Or as sure as God's my judge I'm going to shoot little pieces off of you until you fall apart!'

Fischer lifted his arms even further up: they were almost extended horizontally away from his body, a clear signal that he had no intention of using the gun in the holster at his side.

'I'm not goin' to draw,' he confirmed, his voice shaking. 'You people are witnesses. I'm not drawin', Dick!'

'Pity,' the kid said. His voice was almost conversational, reasonable. For a moment Fischer was fooled by it and the tension went out of him like air from a balloon but even as it did he froze, hardly breathing. The kid had flipped the battered Navy Colt out of the cutaway holster and in one sweet smooth movement he lined up the hexagonal barrel, its bore gaping unwaveringly at a spot in the centre of Fischer's forehead. 'Reckon I'll just have to shoot you down like a mad dog,' Dick Webb said dispassionately, his tone that of a man about to kill a snake. 'Which about describes you anyway.'

Fischer's eyes widened in real panic now. There was no question that the kid meant what he said and the triple click as the gun was cocked sounded like thunder in the silence of the room. Nobody moved: it was like some strange tableau, the long empty wooden bar with Fischer at the end, the tables and the seated men on his right, every face fixed on the boy standing in the centre of the sawdusted floor, his eyes as cold as the inside of an iceberg. A chair scraped softly as someone sitting towards the rear of the saloon shifted uneasily, conscious of being close to the possible line of fire. All the kid had to do was lift his thumb and Joe Fischer was as dead as Moses.

'*Webb!*'

The voice was flat, harsh, peremptory, used to being obeyed. Everyone in the Silver King recognised it and so did the kid. He froze: not turning his head, not moving his eyes from the cringing figure before him whose naked fear was falling away to be replaced with an expression of almost incredulous relief. The people in the saloon still watched Webb. They could see him thinking about what to do next as clearly as if there was a window in his skull. If he lifted his thumb Joe Fischer would die. But so would he: because the man who had spoken his name would kill him without hesitation or compunction.

Tall, thin, grey-haired, dressed in a spotless white shirt, dark pants and vest, soft shining leather boots without spurs, and no hat, Trev Rawley, the town marshal stood in the doorway of the Silver King with a cocked Colt's .44-40 in his hand. His face was tired, deep-etched by lines of experience, indicating he had lived a life in which he'd done most things, seen most things – and cared for practically nothing. There was a silver star on the left lapel of his vest, its dull shine complemented by the glinting nickel-plated sixgun which caught the slanting dust-mote filled beams of sunlight from the window as Trev Rawley gestured with it.

'Ease that hammer down about as slow as you can, Webb,' he said harshly. 'Or I'll put out your light.'

There wasn't any threat in his voice. He said it like someone remarking on the weather, but that didn't mean the kid had any options. Trev Rawley would lay him out cold enough to skate on without a second's thought and there wasn't a man in the room didn't know it – including Dick Webb. His shoulders slumped, and the gun barrel dropped downwards, pointing at the floor, as he eased the hammer down. He just stood there, head hanging, like a kid caught in a lie, face defiant, stance uncertain, watching Trev Rawley come around in front of him, lightfooted, never near enough to be reached by a suddenly-thrown blow or to be caught off-guard by a hideaway gun. Rawley stopped midway between Webb and his intended victim.

'Just let it drop, son,' he said. 'Nice an' easy.'

Webb stood there for a moment, not doing it, not moving, not intending to, and the air went heavy with tension as Rawley cocked his head slightly to one side as much as to say, silently, 'Are you going to try?' Then young Webb abruptly opened his fingers and the gun clunked on the raw pine floor. The concerted sigh as a dozen men let the air out of their lungs was faintly audible.

'Step away from it,' Rawley said. His voice was still completely without any shade of emphasis, as if he'd done this so many times that all it could be was boring. But there was no boredom in his eyes, his stance: he was ready for anything he might have to do. He nodded as the boy took three steps back and to the side, coming up against the bar, head hanging with frustrated shame at being taken so easily.

'All right,' Rawley said harshly. 'What's it all about?'

'Ask him.' Dick Webb jerked his chin at Joe Fischer, who was smiling now, the triumphant smile of a protected bully.

'I asked you,' Rawley said softly. 'And you'd do well to answer me.'

'He's off his head!' Joe Fischer put in hotly, coming forward and standing beside Rawley. 'He came in here and—'

'Shut up.' Rawley's voice was soft, almost caressing. Joe Fischer closed his mouth as if someone had thrown a switch, his face scarlet at this further humiliation. 'Webb, I'm waiting.'

Dick Webb shrugged. There was something in the way he stood, the expression on his face, the way he looked at the marshal, which told the onlookers that the boy figured anything he said now wouldn't matter a hoot in hell. 'You give a damn, Rawley?' he asked. 'You figure Big Ed'll give a damn?'

'Better let me decide that,' was the reply. Rawley gestured with the nickel-plated sixgun. 'I'm still waiting, kid. Spit it out!'

'Okay,' the boy said, wearily, as though he were a parent indulging the persistent marshal. 'Suppose I tell you this . . . this poison toad here is a woman-molester? Suppose I tell you he killed a kid in cold blood? What'll you do, Rawley? Lock him up? Lock up Big Ed Fischer's kid brother?' He let out a mirthless laugh.

'Those are pretty serious charges,' Rawley observed. 'You saying Joe here killed someone? That he attacked a woman someplace?'

'I'm sayin' just that!' snapped Dick Webb. 'Look at his goddamned ugly face – what more proof do you wa—'

That was as far as he got. While he had been speaking, Joe Fischer had edged closer, coming around on Rawley's left side. Now with a scream of inarticulate rage he moved, his cocked fist coming around in a looping haymaker that the youngster had absolutely no chance of ducking. It hit Webb high on the cheekbone near the temple, slamming him against the heavy bar. Eyes sightless, Dick Webb slid down in a disorganised jumble of arms and legs, a slow trickle of bright blood staining the floor beneath his face. Joe Fischer stood over him, legs spraddled wide, fists clenched, waiting. Rawley did nothing: he watched, saying nothing as Dick Webb shook his head, getting unsteadily to his feet. He still had one knee on the ground when Joe Fischer hit him again, square in the face this time, and the boy went back against Rawley's legs, bouncing off on to the sawdusted floor, his face a bright mask of blood from his broken lips. Fischer started forward after the kid, and Webb rolled away instinctively. As he did, his body rolled on to the discarded Navy Colt and his hand closed on it.

Trev Rawley smiled, the smile of a cat that hears the mouse coming, a tight, merciless expectant grin, letting Webb think he had some kind of chance to use the gun. Rawley's own gun was already cocked and lined up to fire and in another half second Dick Webb would have been dead with a bullet through his brain had it not been for the fact that at precisely the moment Rawley's gun came level a shot smashed out from the corner of the room.

The bullet ripped the gun out of Rawley's hand, spinning it away across the bar. It hit the wall and fell to the ground, still cocked. He whirled to face the threat even as Joe Fischer's hand darted in almost reflex action towards his own holstered gun.

'*Don't you!*'

The tall man who held the smoking gun didn't raise his voice, but there was something in the tone, the way the words were spoken, that touched a secret place in Fischer and made him jerk his hand away from the gun as if it had suddenly become poisonous. A look of puzzlement instantaneously touched his face, as if realising how pronounced his reaction had been, he could not understand why. He glared at the intruder, who now stepped clear of the crowd, coming around towards Fischer and Rawley. The latter watched imperturbably, kneading his numbed fingers with his right hand. He saw a big, tall man, wide-shouldered and cold-eyed, tanned as dark as an Indian, the long brown hair streaked and sunbleached, dressed in conventional range clothes: dark, well-worn Levi's, a decent wool shirt, good quality boots. A stranger, passing through, Rawley thought. Obviously doesn't know what he's getting into. But, he warned himself, he can shoot. Any man who can shoot a sixgun accurately enough to smack a gun out of another man's hand twenty feet away is no pilgrim.

'And who the hell might you be?' Fischer was asking, getting a sneer into his voice as he came to the same conclusion as Rawley – without the inbuilt caution of the lawman.

'Might be the Queen of Sheba,' was the cold reply. 'But I'm not. Name's Angel. Frank Angel.'

'Angel?' Rawley said, frowning, trying to place it. He knew most of them. But he'd never heard the name of Frank Angel before. So: not a notch-cutter.

'Angel!' Joe Fischer over-reacted. 'Well, that's rich. An' pretty apt – about what you're li'ble to end up as if you don't put up that gun!' He turned to the bartender, who had risen from his hideout below the bar when the sixgun had skittered to a fully-cocked stop not six inches from his trembling toes. 'Tell him what he's pokin' his nose into, Luskam!' The bartender, Luskam – actually the nominal owner of the Silver King – was a wiry, moustached, white-haired man with the smooth skin and clear eyes of a tee-totaller. He nodded eagerly.

'He's right, mister,' he affirmed. 'It's—'

'Trouble,' Angel said. 'Don't tell me, it always is.'

'Listen,' Luskam said, nervously. 'You're a stranger in town. You don't – you know who this is?' He nodded towards Joe Fischer.

'You give the snakes names in these parts?' Angel asked, coldly. His eyes flicked to Rawley, who was still watching, assessing, waiting. 'What kind of lawman are you, anyway? You were going to shoot down the boy without giving him any sort of chance at all!'

Rawley lifted his shoulders and let them down, as though that were answer enough. Then he lifted his chin.

'Listen, friend,' he said. 'Luskam's giving you it straight. You've gotten into deep water here.'

'I can swim,' Angel said shortly. 'And I'm not your friend.'

Rawley sighed, as though dealing with a stubborn child to whom he would give one more chance before his patience was exhausted.

'Listen. Listen to me, now. Step out of this while you can. My advice—'

'Is probably about the same quality as your peace-officering,' Angel said. 'You, kid—' this to Dick Webb. 'You're not saying much.'

'Not much to say,' Webb replied. 'Except thanks.'

'Save it,' Angel said. 'You want to step around behind me and sort of get by the door, there?'

Dick Webb nodded, sidling around behind Rawley and waiting there as Angel lifted the gun from Joe Fischer's holster and flipped it over behind the bar. It smacked against a wooden crate with a solid thud as Angel stepped around Rawley and moved towards the door. Never got anywhere near where he could be struck or jumped, never once took his eyes off either of us, never once let the sixgun barrel waver an inch: no, certainly not a pilgrim, Rawley thought. Lawman? Professional gun? No matter: bad news whatever he was.

'You better get long gone out of here, friend,' he said to Angel, letting no trace of threat come into his tone, making it a statement of simple fact. 'You'll be in bad trouble if you don't. And I mean bad.'

'I'll bet you do,' Angel said levelly. 'Do I have to keep reminding you I'm not your friend?'

Over his shoulder he asked Dick Webb a question. The youngster nodded.

'Outside,' he said. 'At the hitch rail.'

'Good,' Angel said. 'Mine's the lineback dun with the bedroll. Get on yours and unhitch mine ready. I'll be right along.'

He turned to face Rawley and Joe Fischer.

'Some advice for you, *friend*: stay put!'

'There's no place for you to run, Webb!' Joe Fischer screeched. 'My brothers will take you both apart in strips. You hear me? Strips!'

Angel looked at Rawley and shook his head sadly.

'Why is it always the ones with the least guts who make the most noise?' he asked, rhetorically, certainly not expecting the lawman to answer. Then he gave Dick Webb a nod, and the younger man backed through the batwings as Angel stepped back.

As he did so, a hugely-built man who had been standing just to one side of the doorway swept his hamlike hand in a brutal felling chop. The sixgun clenched in it hit Dick Webb behind the ear with a sound like an axe biting into a log, and the boy went out off the porch, driving into the dirt of the street face down even as Angel, alerted by the sudden change of Rawley's expression, the bright grinning anticipation of Joe Fischer's face, whirled to meet the threat. He was too late and he knew it, but he kept on going anyway. The big man with the gun in his hand had everything going for him. Superior weight, height, reach, added to the head-start offered by the advantage of surprise against Angel's superb reflexes. The barrel of the sixgun smacked across Angel's temple and he went careening backwards into the saloon, lurching into one of the tables, off which he bounced to the floor face down. Even half conscious he was instinctively moving to protect himself as he tried to get up, but Rawley was already beside him, both hands clenched together. He swung them up to the left behind his shoulder, the way a man hefts an axe, and then brought them clubbing down with all his strength on the base of Angel's neck. Angel went flat hard smashing down on the grubby saw-dusted floor with a crash that shook the room and set bottles jingling on the shelves behind the bar. Then Rawley looked up at the big man who had come inside the saloon now and was standing spraddle legged, hands on his hips, staring down at the supine form of Frank Angel, a frown knitting his heavy brows. Then he looked up at the marshal, and an ugly grin formed on his beefy face.

'Rawley,' he said. 'That's a drink you owe me!'

Trev Rawley grinned like a shark, and gestured with the fallen Angel's sixgun at two men standing nearby.

'Get Doug Boyd and George Aitken at the jail. Give them a hand. Get this—' he kicked Angel's unconscious form, '—and the other one across there. Lock 'em up. I'll be by presently.'

The two men hastened to do Rawley's bidding and within a couple of minutes, the two deputies had manhandled Angel's inert form out of the place, dragging the unconscious man by the heels like a sack of potatoes. When the batwings had stopped flapping, Trev Rawley bellied up to the bar, rapping on its surface with a coin. As if it were a signal, conversation burst from the men in the room, each of them watching the trio at the bar warily and careful of every word they spoke. There was no sound of sympathy for Dick Webb or the mysterious stranger who'd helped him. Anyone who went up against the Fischers had it coming to him: everyone knew that.

'Name your poison, Ed,' Trev Rawley grinned.

Big Ed Fischer, oldest, smartest and hardest of the trio, smiled back and slapped the marshal on the shoulder.

'I'll take a whiskey,' he said loudly. 'And I'll take a big one!'

CHAPTER THREE

The Department of Justice had a rule: never get into anything you can't get out of. Everyone who worked in the big, echoing old building in Washington knew it and observed it for a very simple reason – it was a damned sensible rule. Frank Angel reflected ruefully on this as he surveyed the cramped cell in which he was now painfully sitting up. After all his training, all the experience they had pumped into him, he should have known better than to walk straight into a whipsawing that had first, nothing to do with him and second, even less to do with the Justice Department. He didn't even know the rights and wrongs – if any – of the matter. He had just jumped in blind, and now he was stuck in this sweltering box with a head that was throbbing as if there were small men inside with rubber hammers. Serves me right, he thought. I shouldn't have been here at all. If his horse had not thrown a shoe as he came up along the road leading north towards Raton, he would have passed Fischer's Crossing without even seeing it. He was on his way back to Washington, passing through, going home with a job finished and – no doubt – another one waiting. He'd left the Department's senior Special Investigator and his own superior, Angus Wells, lying convalescent in the military hospital at Fort Union. The mad schemes of Rob Denniston which had brought them both out to New Mexico lay buried forever with the madman who had conceived them.*

Still, he consoled himself, there was no way – given that he had to be in that saloon taking a drink at that precise moment – that he could have sat still and watched the cold-eyed Rawley cut down the kid in cold blood. What he hadn't yet figured out was why the rest of the people in the saloon had been willing to sit still and watch their marshal

* related in *Trap Angel* (Sphere Books)

cold-cock the kid: He raised his head and looked across at Dick Webb, who was sitting on the edge of the cot on the other side of the cell, face empty, thoughts a thousand miles away.

'Dick,' Angel said gravely. 'You look pretty much about the way I feel.'

'Mister Angel,' Webb said, coming out of his reverie. 'You're no oil painting yourself.'

He was right. Angel's scalp was torn and bloody behind his ear where the wicked force of Big Ed Fischer's ripping sixgun barrel had hit it. His shirt collar was stiff and matted with dried blood, while his face was dusty and scratched. The front of his body was relatively clean but from hip to shoulder at the back his clothes were covered with street dirt and horse droppings, rubbed and torn against his shoulder blades.

'Looks like we were dragged in here by the feet,' Angel commented. 'You feeling all right?'

'I guess so,' Dick Webb said, doubtfully.

'You see who it was hit us?'

'Yeah,' Dick said. 'Big Ed. Big Ed Fischer. The oldest of the Fischer boys. You met the youngest one in the Silver King.'

'And took no pleasure from it,' Angel said. 'How come this town is so buffaloed, kid?'

'That's the Fischers too,' Webb told him.

'Tell me,' suggested Angel, leaning back against the wall. He winced as his skinned shoulders touched the raw surface of the adobe.

'Not much to tell,' Webb shrugged. 'There are three of them. Ed, Mike and Joe. Ed's the oldest, the biggest, and the meanest. He runs things: the ranch up in the Arabelas – the Flyin' Fish – gives the orders. Spends a lot of his time in Santa Fe, hobnobbin' with the politicians down there. Folks around here seem to think he might run for Governor one day.'

'And Mike?'

'Mike's the muscle, the blunt instrument. If Ed wants

somebody leaned on, somebody roughed up, somebody warned off – Mike does it. He's not as big as Ed, not as tall I mean – but he's built like an adobe outhouse and you couldn't break his skull with a double-bitted axe.'

'That makes Joe the runt of the litter.'

'Runt's not the word I'd use, although it's near,' Dick Webb said vehemently. 'He wouldn't be tolerated by anyone in these parts for a second if he wasn't a Fischer. He runs up bills he never pays, borrows stuff he has no intention of returning, drinks like a fish. Just a waster – never does an honest day's work in his life.'

'How come you took out after him?'

'Personal matter,' was the succinct reply, and Angel didn't push. The boy would tell him when he was ready to. Not before.

'The town's named for the family, of course,' he hazarded.

'Right,' Webb said. 'Old Michael J. He settled this valley back in the 'sixties, right after the War Between the States. Built up one of the biggest spreads in the Territory – nearly as big as Chisum's down in Lincoln county. Got his beef from Charlie Goodnight himself. Built up trade with the Army. Used to be an Army post about sixty miles north: old Camp Elliott. Knew every man jack there – from bugle-boy to commanding officer. Sold them all their beef, horses too. Then he built a saloon down here, far enough away to keep it respectable, still nearer than anything else. Got all their trade, all their leave money. Soldiers would come down here, stay up at the Flying Fish, drink at the Silver King, go back to Camp Elliott busted – but happy.'

'Smart operator,' Angel commented.

'Sure he was. They broke the mould after they made Michael Joseph Fischer. He pretty near built this town single handed. General store, saloon, this jail we're in. Livery stable across the street. He was planning on a hotel when he died.'

'When was that?'

'Same year the Army abandoned Camp Elliott – 'seventy four. Like he didn't want to be around any more. The town had grown up around him; he didn't want to see it decline and blow away.'

'It didn't quite do that,' Angel pointed out.

'Not quite,' Webb said. 'But there aren't many people left here now. Old Luskam, who runs the Silver King, the Williamses at the north end of the street, couple of dozen men who one way and another owe their livelihood to the Fischers. Three or four small ranches way on south of town. And that's about it. Fischer's Crossing is sort of the centre of the universe to them: which tends to mean they don't figure to upset the Fischers.'

'And you?'

'My old man had a small place up in the hills, maybe ten miles east of town on the Rio Abajo. There are two rivers. The Rio Arriba runs almost due southwest. The Flying Fish is on the Rio Arriba, fifteen miles north of town. The two rivers meet just outside town.'

'Hence Fischer's Crossing?'

'Correct. When my old man died, a couple of years ago, he left the ranch to me and my sister. Susie's just a kid, eighteen. We do the best we can, but making the place pay isn't easy. I have to drive my cattle down to the Panhandle or over the hellangone to Clayton to get a decent price. Or do like the sheep around here and hand them over to the Fischers at whatever price they're prepared to pay me.'

'How come?'

'They've got the beef contract for the Reservation – that's why Ed's so thick with the politicos in the Capital. It's the only major beef market this side of the Sierra.'

'You the only one drives his own beef to market?'

'Uhuh. Everyone else just buckles under to Big Ed. The extra profit doesn't run to enough to warrant the risk.'

'Risk?'

'Nobody could prove this, of course,' Dick Webb said. 'But old Gus Parrack who's got a ranch southwest of town once decided to run a herd down as far as Fort Union, try his luck. Took three men with him. One night their herd was stampeded. One of the riders was killed – could have been an accident, of course. Took them three days to round up the steers. While they were out hunting them up old Gus was beaten half to death back in the camp. Never would say who did it. Just got back on his pony and headed uphill to here. Damned near dead when he got back. He never even talked about it again.'

'You figure it was the Fischers?'

'Damned sure of it,' Webb said hotly. 'Who the hell else would it be?'

'Good question,' Angel said. 'Except for one thing: why haven't they hit you?'

'Two reasons, I guess. One is – was, rather – that my old man and Michael J. were friends. So there's a kind of amnesty thing. Besides I don't run enough head for it to make much difference. The second reason is my sister.'

Angel raised his eyebrows, but said nothing; the expression on the boy's face indicated that the sister was close to whatever had caused him to come looking for Joe Fischer with blood in his eye.

'Old Michael J. always hoped that when Susie grew up she'd marry one of his boys, unite the two ranches into one huge one. Well,' he ended grimly, 'that's over now too.'

'You want to tell me about it, kid?'

'No,' Dick Webb said. 'I don't want to get into that. Not yet awhile.' His face was stony, eyes far off again, and Angel got to his feet, stretching his arms until they creaked.

'God, I'm as stiff as a gunbarrel,' he said. His outstretched fingers just brushed the ceiling of their cell. There wasn't any more room in it than there had to be, he thought. The walls were just far enough apart to allow room for two cots with a walking space between them. A bucket stood in one corner: the complete sanitary arrangements. The walls were of unpainted adobe, solid and thick. The door was of oak and bound with thick strips of heavy steel. Short of dynamiting their way out, there was no likelihood of their escaping.

He sat down again, his thoughts sombre. Stumbling into Fischer's Crossing he had encountered a situation which was hardly unique out West. The man who controlled the

Army's beef contracts, or the supply of beef to Reservation Indians, or both, controlled the only real money there was these days after the big depression of '73. Local commerce depended on him. He was the machine. And because he was, he took two bites of everything: once when it was sold, once when it was bought. You sold your stock to the machine for the price it arbitrarily decided to pay. Since without the contract, you couldn't sell the stock yourself, you had to take their price. Now, nominally, you had money to buy enough supplies to keep you in business for another year. But the only place you could buy it was in the store controlled or owned by the machine. At their prices. Of course, you could always get into a wagon and drive a couple of hundred miles to a town where the prices might just be a few cents cheaper. It would mean neglecting your work for the best part of a week, though. So who had the time, let alone the inclination? It was easier to go along with the machine, which never squeezed you quite hard enough to kill. Old Michael J. Fischer had known what he was about, Angel thought. He'd picked his location perfectly.

'Anybody ever bucked the Fischers this hard before?' Angel asked the boy.

'Nope,' Webb said. 'Soon after old Michael J. died, Ed brought in Trev Rawley. He came up here from Texas – Fort Griffin, I heard – and settled in as town marshal.'

'I wouldn't have thought there was that much for him to do?'

'He keeps the town in line. Also makes sure that any unwelcome drifters keep drifting. He may do other – work for the Fischers. I don't know. All I know is he's sudden death.'

'Figured that,' Angel said softly.

'Oh, one or two of the folks in town don't back off from him, or the Fischers,' Dick Webb said. 'But it's token defiance. Old Billy Luskam, who runs the Silver King. Doc Day, Bry Leavey that runs the store. Now and again they're inclined to speak up and be damned to the Fischers. But they're pretty powerless.'

'Which makes you the exception again,' Angel pointed out.

'Well, I had damned good reason to be the exception,' growled Dick Webb. 'Hell, Angel, I reckon if anyone's entitled to know about it, you are. You wanted to know why I came in after Joe Fischer. All right, I'll tell you. I was out on the range all night, slept at one of the line camps. My sister was supposed to ride out around midday, bring me some food. She didn't turn up. Around two, I forked my pony and got on back to the ranch in case there was something wrong. I got back about four o'clock. Shouted for Susie but there was no answer. You know how you get that prickle on the back of your neck that tells you something is wrong? Really bad wrong?'

Angel nodded. He knew the feeling, all right. He'd been fourteen when he first experienced it, hiding in a tree while the Union soldiers who had killed his father went into the house after his screaming mother. Just as he'd experienced the sudden absence of any sense of reality or fear as he had gone into the house and killed the soldier on the top of the stairs who was grinning as he fastened his pants, then gone into the bedroom and killed the other one who was holding his mother down.

'There was only the four of us out there,' he heard the boy continue. 'Susie an' me, an old Mexican woman who cooks for us, and her son Pedro to look after the horses, mend fences. Just a kid, fourteen, but he does a man's work. Anyway, I rode up, there was no sign of anyone. Pedro usually comes out front to get the horses. Nobody around. I ran into the house. You . . . you should have seen . . . '

His voice broke for a moment and he swallowed noisily, looking up at the ceiling and stretching his face to keep the angry tears out of his eyes. 'The old woman was in the living room with Pedro dead in her arms. She'd carried him inside. She was sitting there alone, rocking the dead kid in her arms. Her eyes were as empty as the pits of hell. She didn't even see me. I ran around, kicking the doors open. Then I found Susie. She was – oh, God *damn* that sonofabitch!'

He pounded an ineffective fist into the mattress of the cot.

Angel got up slowly, touching Webb's arm lightly, just a small hint of sympathy for he knew that too much would open up floodgates which Dick Webb was trying desperately to keep closed. He went towards the door, examining it minutely for long minutes, as if it were some rare, newly-discovered manuscript in an exotic, long-forgotten language, and stayed there until the kid had a chance to get hold of himself again.

'He beat her, Mister Angel,' the boy said softly. 'He beat her like a cutnose squaw and then he ripped the clothes off her and took her on the floor like an animal. He killed a fourteen-year-old kid who came running to help her. Susie told me. She was in poor shape, but she told me what had happened. She tried to fight him off, screamed, kicked, scratched. But he hit her. He hit her with his fists, man! Pedro came running through the doorway with his old gun in his hand. An old Dragoon Colt that would've knocked him down if he'd tried to fire it. Fischer shot him down like a coyote.'

He trembled as he spoke, the anger burning up in him again as he relived his experience.

'I don't even remember getting Susie and Deluvina into the wagon, but I must have done it. I was just so blind mad.'

'Where'd you send them?' Angel asked.

'Over to our nearest neighbours, Gus Parrack's place down to the south of the Rio Abajo. There wasn't anything I could do for either of them. Except what I did. I got on my horse and I came after Joe Fischer. I couldn't think of anything except wanting to kill him and I wanted that so badly I could taste it.'

'Which is where I came in,' Angel said. 'Your sister going to be all right?'

'I don't know. I guess so, but I don't know. Dorothy Parrack's a good woman. And Deluvina. They'll look after her.'

'Maybe we can get someone to send the doctor out there,' Angel said. 'When and if our friend the marshal ever shows up. Wonder what he's got in store for us?'

'Nothing good, you can bet on that,' Dick Webb said. 'But he'll have to check with Big Ed first. It's Big Ed's town. He'll decide what happens.'

Angel nodded, but said nothing. He'd not really been asking a question, just making soothing noises. He knew damned well that it was Ed Fischer's town, and he wasn't at all sanguine about his or the boy's prospects in the immediate future. Whatever, it wouldn't be good news. So he prowled the cramped confines of their prison, tapping the walls, testing the door by putting his weight against it, checking the barred window. Nothing moved, nothing sagged, nothing crumbled. The place was built like a blockhouse, and even though Frank Angel had one or two weapons hidden about his person that only the minutest of searches would have revealed, they were not designed to make holes in solid oak doors or three-foot thick adobe walls. They might give him a fighting chance in other ways, but here they were worse than useless. There wasn't even a judas window on the door.

'I could've told you not to bother,' Dick Webb said, as Angel sat down on his cot. 'Those walls were built to stand up to anything. Even the window's too small for a man to crawl through, supposin' he could pry all the bars loose.'

'Just making sure,' Angel said.

'Uhuh,' Webb replied. 'The only place built stronger than the jail is the Flyin' Fish ranchhouse itself.' He tapped the unpainted wall with a knuckle. 'Remember what I told you about old Camp Elliott? This is some of it.'

Angel shrugged, but before he could make any verbal reply, they heard the sound of heavy footsteps outside their cell door, and the jangling of keys. The lock rattled, and then the door swung outwards to reveal Trev Rawley standing in the hallway, arms akimbo, a faint smile touching his saturnine face. Behind him stood two burly men, both armed with riot guns. Angel's eyes automatically checked the weapons off: twin-barrel Greeners, sawn off at eight inches, butts shortened to pistol grips and taped for comfort and steady hold. Each barrel would be holding a cartridge with nine heavy buckshot slugs – blue whistlers, as they were called – which would quite literally cut a man's body in half at this kind of range. Rawley saw his glance and smiled like a shark.

'You're right,' he said. 'So no tricks. Let's go.'

'Go where?' Angel asked.

'You'll see, my impetuous friend,' Rawley told him. 'And this time, don't do anything as silly as you tried in the Silver King. My two boys here are the twitchy-fingered sort. They pull them triggers, it's liable to make your eyes water some.'

'You got your orders from Big Ed, then, Trev,' Dick Webb commented flatly. If the menacing barrels of the riot guns fazed him, he gave no sign of it, his chin thrust out angrily towards the marshal. Rawley didn't bite at Webb's bait, though.

'You might say,' was his only reply.

'What you got in mind, Rawley?' Angel asked.

'Get on out here and you'll be on your way to finding out,' Rawley said, jerking his head to emphasise the words. 'Head on over to the saloon.'

The two men looked at each other and shrugged. Angel led the way out into the corridor, and Rawley preceded them into the outer office, the two deputies bringing up the rear.

'Should be an interestin' trial,' Rawley commented, throwing away the comment. Dick Webb stopped in his tracks, mouth open, ignoring the prodding barrel that the deputy stuck into his kidneys.

'Trial?' he shouted. 'What the hell trial you talking about, Rawley?'

'Oh,' Rawley said, turning slowly, a thin smile forming around his mouth. 'Couple of smart old boys like you oughta be able to figure that one out.'

'Fischer, you mean?' Angel said. 'You're trying Joe Fischer?'

Rawley put a look of studied surprise on his face.

'Joe?' he said. 'What would we want to try Joe for?'

'Killing Pedro Martinez out at my place, that's what!' Dick Webb snapped. 'An'—'

'Hold on there!' Rawley said sharply, raising a hand in the *stop* signal. 'You off your head or something, Webb?'

'Goddammit you know I'm not, Rawley!' Dick Webb said.

Rawley shook his head.

'Then quit actin' as if you are, son,' he told the youngster. 'Joe Fischer hasn't even been out of town for three days. And there's half a dozen men willing to swear to it.'

The sardonic smile returned as he saw Dick Webb's anger turn to speechless disgust.

'So the trial's for us?' Angel asked, softly.

'Right you are,' Rawley said.

'I've seen some cheap imitations of lawmen in my day, Rawley,' Angel said, a cutting edge of contempt in his voice that brought high spots of colour to the lawman's cheekbones, 'but you're something else.'

For a moment, Rawley fought with the urge to retaliate, hit back physically. His hand clawed over the sixgun butt at his hip, but then he took a deep breath and relaxed, his hand unclenching.

'Sticks and stones, Angel,' he said, making himself grin. 'On your way!'

CHAPTER FOUR

There were plenty of people on the street now.

During the night and morning of their incarceration, the word had spread around town like wildfire that Dickie Webb and the stranger had tried to take on the Fischer boys and been smacked into the slammer. Everyone wanted to take a look at them, and everyone wanted to see the trial they'd heard was going to take place. Might be that the two prisoners were foolhardy brave, might be it was about time somebody went up against the Fischers, might be that most decent men would be glad to see them toppled: but what could anyone do on his own? So they clustered outside the jail in the flat sunshine, up and down the boardwalks on both sides of the street, a strange silence holding them, making the bright morning seem somehow ominous.

None of the men watching met the contemptuous eyes of young Dick Webb, Angel noted. Himself they favoured with the curious stare of people confronted by an unknown species of animal.

He ignored them, getting his first proper look at the town. When he'd first ridden in to Fischer's Crossing, it had just been another wide spot in the trail, another town like all the other towns along the way. You tended to get so you didn't see them. They all had the same shanty false fronts, the same curlicued lettering and ornate woodwork concealing the shacks behind them. And Fischer's Crossing was no lovelier than it had to be.

At the southern edge of town was a wooden bridge crossing the stone-strewn sandy bed of the Rio Arriba, its level almost nil at this time of year. One or two scattered stone or adobe houses, a frame shack on this side, a flat-roofed hovel on the other fringed the wide, empty street before you encountered the first building of any appreciable size on the right: the livery stable. Up the street perhaps twenty yards stood the Silver King, with the jail's L-shaped hulk directly opposite it. Next to the saloon was the long, porch-shaded barrack-like store which catered to such needs as the inhabitants had or could afford. Opposite it was the eats house, run by an elderly Chinese whose name no one had ever found out. A few more houses skirted the street, with others further back on the higher ground above the town and alongside the Rio Arriba. The cribs occupied by the girls who worked in the Silver King were in broken, litter-strewn ground in back of the livery stable and to the south of the saloon. Fischer's Crossing was just about all it had to be and not a plank more.

Inside the saloon, the tables had been cleared back against the walls, with rows of chairs facing towards the rear of the saloon. Benches were set up on the southern wall opposite the bar. All were crammed with men, and even one or two women, whose subdued speculation raised an audible buzz as the two prisoners were marched down the aisle between the rows of chairs in the centre of the room towards the cleared space in back, where a square table and a bentwood chair had been placed. On the left of the table, four chairs, two by two. The prisoners were led to these and told to sit down, while the deputies sat in the chairs behind them, the riot guns laid conspicuously across their knees. Rawley took a chair in the empty row in front, his face as expressionless as the furniture.

Angel could feel the stares of the onlookers on the back of his neck, but he kept his own face empty, impassive. There were people behind him who had seen Rawley try to murder the boy in the saloon in which they were now sitting. There was no point in expecting any help from them. Or anyone else, come to that, he reflected. His reverie was interrupted by Rawley, who stood up and rapped on the table with the barrel of his sixgun.

'All rise!' the lawman said loudly, and the people in the audience shuffled to their feet, open grins on some of their faces. Heads turned to see the man who had come in through the batwings and was now making his way towards the table. He was a wobbling, lard-faced old man of about seventy, his grubby shirt collarless, his face stubbled and unshaven. His eyes were narrowed, the weak mouth querulous, his expression the rheumy vacancy of the compulsive drinker. His old black clawhammer coat looked as if it had been slept in. In a cowshed.

A rumpot, Angel thought as the old man fumbled his way into the chair and lifted his watery eyes to look around. The kind that will fish in a spittoon for a dollar to buy his morning set-up and then hang about a saloon all day on the off-chance of a free drink or a simple chore in exchange for one. The shifty eyes met Angel's, flickered away quickly, fixed themselves as malevolently upon Dick Webb and flickered away as quickly when the youngster looked up.

'This court is now in session!' Rawley said loudly and sat down.

The old man nodded, but before he could say anything, every head in the place turned and there was a hum of anticipation in the crowded room that Angel knew could only mean one thing: the Fischer boys had arrived. Now he saw them coming down the gangway, heard one or two men call a quietly respectful greeting. If either of the two men coming towards the table heard any of these greetings, they made no acknowledgement, vocal or physical. Not so much as a curt nod.

'The shorter of the two is Mike,' Dick Webb muttered out of the side of his mouth. 'Ed's the one with the high style.'

Angel hardly needed to be told. Mike Fischer was squat, barrel-shaped, an ugly, powerful man, his face a broken, scarred, blurrier version of his brother's. He looked like what he was: a man who could enforce and would enjoy enforcing his brother's decisions. But it was Big Ed himself who caught the attention and held it.

He was a big man and a handsome man, and he knew it and was proud of it. Well over six feet tall, broad as a young bull across the shoulders, Ed Fischer was in the prime of his life and looked as if he was enjoying every moment of it. His lips were thick and sensual, his eyes deep and dark and liquid, a hint of cruelty in the lines at their outer edges. On him sat that indefinable air of confidence which comes from many years of being obeyed without question, from a knowledge of superior and unchallenged intellect, from a decade or more of fine food and fine clothes and fine whiskey which, even if they had thickened him slightly around the middle, combined to exude from the man as power, strength, confidence. Unlike his brothers, and in spite of the heavy hard heat of the sun, he affected a dark broadcloth suit which fitted him the way that only a hand-made suit will hang on a man and which, despite its film of traildust, was obviously expensive, Eastern-cut. A heavy, tooled leather gunbelt sagged around his waist. His Frontier Model Colt was nickle plated and had ivory butt-plates.

Without looking either to the right or the left, Big Ed stalked up the gangway and sat down heavily in the chair next to Trev Rawley, nodding briefly to the old man at the table, giving his permission to begin. Mike Fischer sat meekly beside him, head hunched into his shoulders, eyes glaring from beneath the beetling brows. Angel saw Joe Fischer now for the first time; the youngest of the brothers took his place next to Mike, smiling and nodding at people who had said hello to him as he went past. Dick Webb nudged Angel, pointing with his chin at a pale-skinned man with yellow-white hair that curled down over the collar of his dark blue shirt. The man was moving unobtrusively across the room towards the deserted bar; he looked about fifty at first glance, but then Angel saw that he was much younger – no more than thirty. The impression of age was created by the withered, whitened skin of the albino, that curious genetic mistake which produced an almost transparent texture in skin, hair, eyes. The man was thin, frail-looking, perhaps five feet seven in height. He moved soft and catlike on small feet.

'Francey King,' Webb whispered. 'Fischer's foreman.'

Angel nodded, noting the tied-down holsters, twin eagle-bill Colt's .38 double action revolvers, the wide leather gunbelt with its silver conchos, subtle Navajo patterns beaten into them matching the tooling of the leather. He had no time himself for fancy gun rigs or for double-action pistols either, but that was not to say that he would ever underestimate a man who used them. The tied-down fancy holsters, the gleaming nickelplated guns, were a sign plain for anyone who cared to read it: saying, '*killer*'. Foreman, King might be. Hired gunman he most decidedly was. Any man who wore King's kind of outfit – the dark clothes, the dramatically flat-crowned Stetson – did so from a need to be noticed, to set themselves apart, to be challenged. This pink-eyed one looked to be about as poisonous as the breed came.

'Court'll come to order!' the fat old man at the table wheezed. The buzz of conversation which had resumed after the Fischers took their seats fell to a murmur and Rawley got to his feet. He took his place in the cleared space in front of the table.

'Court's in session, Judge George Regenvogel presiding!' he announced.

'Judge,' Angel heard Webb mutter contemptuously.

'Bring the first prisoner before the bench,' the judge said.

There was a stir of anticipation as Angel was prodded to his feet by the shotgun barrel and shepherded forward in front of the makeshift bench.

The old man bent his rheumy gaze on the tall man in front of him.

'Your full name?'

'Frank Angel.'

'Where you from, Angel?'

'You mean originally, or lately?'

'Don't get smart, Angel,' Rawley growled, stepping forward. 'Just answer.'

'Washington,' Angel said. 'Lately I've been working down Kiowa way.'

'Doing what?'

'Anything that came along.'

'I will not tolerate impertinence, my friend,' warned Regenvogel. 'Do you hear?'

'I hear,' Angel said. 'And I'm not your friend.'

The deputy behind him again poked the shotgun barrel into his back, making him lurch forward, slightly off balance. For a moment, Angel's temper flared and he half-turned, only to see Rawley watching him expectantly, a thin waiting smile on his mouth. Angel took a deep breath and turned to face the judge again.

'I was guarding a . . . special shipment going from Animas to Fort Union,' he said. It was near enough to the truth. The fact that the 'shipment' had been the President of the United States, Ulysses S. Grant, was another matter.

'What brings you to these parts, Angel?' asked Regenvogel.

'Just passing through,' Angel told him. 'On my way home.'

The old man looked at Trev Rawley and licked his stubble-shaded lips.

'What charges you bringing here, Trev?' he asked.

Rawley grinned like a mongoose and held up a hand with the fingers spread. He began ticking off as he spoke.

'Assault with a deadly weapon, one; felonious assault on duly appointed officer of law, two; resisting arrest, three; interfering with officer inna course of duty, four; inciting civil disturbance, five – hell, any of those would do, judge. But we'll go with attempted murder!'

A malicious little smile played around the corners of the old man's prune-lipped mouth as Rawley spoke. He looked at Angel from beneath his brows and then his tricky gaze slid over towards Ed Fischer. Fischer's nod was almost imperceptible; but only almost. Angel saw it and his lip curled.

'Any witnesses?' Regenvogel asked of the marshal.

'Plenty,' Rawley said. 'You want me to call them?'

'Let's see about that,' the judge said. 'Prisoner, how do you plead: guilty or not guilty?'

'You mean it makes a difference?' Angel asked, making his mock surprise huge and clownish. There were one or two involuntary snickers from the well of the court, quickly stifled. Dick Webb laughed out loud, his laughter ceasing in a gasp of pain as one of the deputies jammed the barrel of his shotgun into the kid's ribs.

'Allus liked a fellow with plenty of spunk,' said Regenvogel, no sign of liking or admiration visible on his sunken face. 'I'll bear it in mind when I pronounce sentence.'

'You're ready to pronounce sentence already,' Angel observed. 'Without even letting me speak in my own defence?'

Regenvogel cocked his head like an intelligent lizard.

'Think it'll make a difference?' he mimicked. This time the courtroom exploded with laughter, and the old man's shoulders shook as he looked towards the seated Fischers for approval. His laughter sounded like a rattlesnake in a box full of old newspapers.

'Probably no damned difference at all!' snapped Angel, stilling the laughter with an angry voice that cut through it, sharp and commanding. 'But I expect to be heard!'

'Go ahead,' Regenvogel shrugged. He leaned back and closed his eyes, an expression of complete disinterest on his face. There were sniggers at this patent indication of boredom with anything the accused might have to say.

'Take it easy, Angel,' Rawley advised softly.

'Easy, hell!' Angel retorted. 'What the hell kind of kangaroo court is this, anyway?'

Regenvogel's eyes snapped open, a mottled flush rising to stain his face. He leaned forward and banged on the table with the flat of his hand.

'Sir!' he screeched, 'You are in contempt of this court!'

'Sir!' Angel told him flatly. 'You're damned right I am!'

'Marshal, sit this man down!' Regenvogel shouted, banging the table again and again, his voice mounting to be heard over the awed mutter of conversation which had started. 'Sit him down! We shall deal with him presently!'

Angel shrugged, not resisting as the deputies jostled him back to his seat. He ignored the glaring eyes of the Fischers: the hell with them. What had just happened was such a breathtaking travesty of judicial procedure that railing against it was like cursing the thunderstorm that was drenching you. It might make you feel better, but it sure as hell wouldn't make you any drier. With protest doomed to failure, and more overt action likely to get not only himself but young Webb killed where they stood, there was nothing to do but sit down and try to control the churning anger inside him.

Now he realised that the deputies had hustled Dick Webb up in front of the old man at the table and he looked up as Regenvogel asked a question.

'You know my name, you old fraud,' Dick Webb said stoutly. 'And you know where I live and what I do for a living. And why I'm here, I don't doubt. Although I reckon you won't want the real truth none.'

'Oh, I don't know about that,' leered the judge. 'Rawley, why is he here?'

'Attempted murder like the other one, judge,' Rawley said. 'Fact is, I reckon young Webb here hired this other one, Angel, to come into town an' try to whipsaw young Joe Fischer for reasons of his own we ain't dug up yet. Lucky for Joe I was around to put the blocks on that.'

This breathtaking distortion brought a shout of anger from Dick Webb, and he turned towards Rawley with his hands clenching into fists, only to stop in mid-turn as the deputy behind him reminded the youngster once again that there were two short barrels of buckshot within an inch of his spine. Webb let it all drain out of him fast, his shoulders coming down from their angry hunch.

'There you go, judge,' Rawley said, gesturing towards Dick Webb. 'Real little cattymount, ain't he? No question he was out to kill Joe Fischer. A dozen men saw him, heard him say he was about to do it.'

'I see,' Regenvogel said. He pursed his lips and steepled his fingers, leaning back in his chair and weighing the matter in such a ham-actor way that it would have been funny in any situation other than this grimly real one. Angel got to his feet, ignoring the deputy behind him.

'Why doesn't one of you ask the kid why he came looking for Fischer?' he shouted. 'Let him tell his side of it!'

'I've heard the kid's side of it, judge,' Rawley said evenly, not taking his eyes off Angel. 'Some cock-and-bull tale about Joe attacking his sister, killing some Mexican kid down at the Flying W. Plain nonsense. I checked with Joe: he tells me he ain't been out of town in three days. Sent a man down to the Webb place. Nobody there. No dead Mexican boys, no beaten-up sisters, nobody at all.'

'I see,' the judge said again. He looked levelly at Dick Webb, whose eyes were on Rawley, looking at the man with a disgust which was almost admiration.

'Well, boy,' Regenvogel said, harshly. 'How do you plead?'

'If you're asking me did I come after Joe Fischer intendin' to kill him like the snivelling skunk that he is, the answer is yes, I did! And I plead guilty as hell to the charge!' snapped Dick Webb. There was a hiss of indrawn breath from the watching spectators as he rapped out the words, which was stilled to a stunned silence as he added 'And if I had a gun in my hand I'd shoot the sonofabitch right now!'

Trying hard, but unsuccessfully, to keep the triumph off his face, Regenvogel turned towards Ed Fischer, who smiled faintly, and gave another of his almost-imperceptible nods. His rheumy eyes swivelled around to fix upon the boy in front of him and he smacked the table with the flat of his hand.

'You stand convicted by your own statement!' he said. 'Duty of this court is to ensure you have no chance to effect the threat you have uttered openly and in such contempt of the law before this bench.' Regenvogel peered towards the spectators in the well of the courtroom.

'In the normal course of events, we would empanel a jury and hear all the evidence in a case of attempted murder. But the prisoner has just made a public confession, admitted not only his guilt, but indicated quite clearly that given the opportunity he will attempt to take the life of Joseph Fischer again. Clearly he must not be given that chance. Is there anyone in the court who wishes to dispute my judgment?'

There wasn't a movement among the spectators. Trev Rawley stood off to one side, his thumbs hooked negligently in his belt, eyes checking every face in the room. By the bar, Francey King was looking about the room eagerly, as though hoping someone might speak up. But no one did. No one was going to buck the assembled might of the Fischers. Regenvogel let the silence build for a few more moments, glaring at the spectators from beneath his tatty eyebrows. Then he made a curt gesture towards Rawley.

'Bring the other one up here as well,' he said.

Angel let his gaze move from face to face. He saw no sign of sympathy, no indication that anyone gave a damn about what was happening.

'Well,' Regenvogel said. 'Anything to say, either of you?'

'Nothing you'd understand,' Angel told him.

'Make the most of your chances for cheap humour, my friend,' Regenvogel said silkily. 'You'll not have many more chances to insult this court.'

'Court?' Dick Webb scoffed. 'Court? I'd rather be tried by drunken Apaches!'

Rawley laid a hand on the boy's shoulder, his fingers near the base of Dick Webb's neck. He appeared to use no strength, but Angel saw the boy's jaw muscles tense, face whiten, as the lawman's steely fingers bit into the nerves, saw the youngster's mouth distort with pain. He started to move involuntarily, but once again the poking shotgun barrels dissuaded him.

'Just . . . be quiet,' Rawley said softly to the boy. '*Sabe*?'

'Rawley,' Angel said. His voice was low, as soft as the lawman's. But something in the tone made the man look up as if he had been stung, his eyes narrowed and wary.

'Leave the boy alone,' Angel said. It was doubtful if anyone other than Rawley knew he had spoken. But the marshal's face paled, lifting his hand away from Dick Webb's shoulder involuntarily. In the moment he did it, his brain told him that there was nothing Angel could possibly do, and he looked at his hand angrily, as though it had deliberately disobeyed him.

Angel wasn't even looking at the marshal now. He had swung around to face Regenvogel, his eyes burning with barely-restrained anger.

'Get on with it, you old fraud,' he snapped. 'I want to see how far you'll go with this charade!'

The deputy behind Angel looked at Rawley and then at Big Ed Fischer, helplessly asking them what to do to shut his prisoner up. The big man nodded, rising easily to his feet and crossing the space between them in two soft, easy strides. He stood beside Frank Angel, lambent fire in the depths of his dark eyes.

'The judge is a friend of mine,' he said softly, warningly.

'I can see that,' Angel replied not troubling to hide his contempt.

He saw Fischer's eyes flicker, saw the shoulder drop, knew what was coming next and realised there wasn't a damned thing he could do about it. He tried as well as he could to ride the blow, but Fischer's smashing, looping swipe caught him high on the temple, and Angel was smacked against the table, a blurring white light blanking out his vision for a moment. He cannoned off the table and down on to his knees on the gritty board floor, shaking his head, trying to clear his vision. Then he felt the touch of cold metal on the side of his throat and he froze. With Rawley's sixgun barrel jammed against his jugular vein, Angel was hauled to his feet, reeling slightly. Rawley gestured impatiently to the other deputy, who grabbed Angel's arms and held him upright in front of the table.

'All right,' hissed Regenvogel, his eyes malign. 'All right! That's quite sufficient evidence for this court! I see no indication that you, Webb, if freed, would not immediately attempt to do again what you have just been prevented from doing. Nor do I see any indication that this saddle-tramp you have hired to help you in your murderous plans would not also again attempt to earn his blood money. Well, we've got our own way of dealing with would-be murderers!' Regenvogel got to his feet and thrust his sallow, sunken face forward across the table, devilish enjoyment dancing in his shifting eyes as he shouted the words, spittle on his blue-tinged lips. 'Marshal – take this little bastard out of here and hang him! And while you're at it hang the other one. Hang Angel!'

CHAPTER FIVE

There was complete and utter silence in the packed saloon.

No one so much as breathed. Regenvogel's words hung in the air like carrion birds circling a fallen animal, almost palpable in their deathly intent. Dick Webb stood rooted to the spot, speechless astonishment written all over his open young face. Even the spectators, who had been expecting exactly what they now heard, were stilled by the old man's outburst, for while it was one thing to use the law to achieve your ends, it was another thing altogether to hang a man for no reason worth the name.

'Damn me,' muttered one man in the centre of the room. 'Someone orta do somethin'.'

'Sure,' agreed his neighbour, smiling sardonically. 'Fly at it, Charlie. See how far you get before that smilin' ghost over there drops you in your tracks.' He pointed with his chin towards Francey King, who was looking their way. The man beside him paled, and shrank down in his chair. It was one thing to contemplate injustice; quite another to fight it. It was obvious everyone in the audience felt pretty much the same way. Nobody spoke. Nobody moved. Nobody protested.

'Take them away!' Regenvogel said, triumph in his voice. He smacked the table with the flat of his hand. 'Court's adjourned!' Angel saw him glance towards Ed Fischer, saw the big man nod. *Satisfactory*. The old man glowed, his tongue touching lips already tasting the implicitly promised alcohol. He smiled; he'd handled it well.

'Hold it!'

Heads turned as if on swivels as Frank Angel spoke, shaking off the supporting hands of the two deputies and drawing himself erect, fighting off the dizziness which had kept him nauseous and reeling while Regenvogel had pronounced his sentence. The two deputies stood back, alarmed, the shotgun barrels coming up. There was something about Angel, some air of assurance, command, that unnerved them slightly. Trev Rawley felt his fingertips touch the butt of his sixgun and frowned in surprise at his own action.

'This court—!' Regenvogel blustered. 'This court is—!'

'About due for a surprise!' Angel said grimly. 'And I'm it.'

'What is this, Angel?' Rawley snapped pushing forward past his deputies.

'Hold your men off while I reach inside my belt, Rawley,' Angel said.

'You do it, it better be very very slow, my friend!' Rawley warned.

Angel shook his head. 'Why does everyone round here call me his friend?' he wondered out loud.

Ed Fischer was leaning forward in his chair, a frown of puzzlement on his face as he watched Angel. People at the back half rose from their seats to see over the heads of the craning spectators in front of them as Angel slid something from the slit pocket inside the belt, something which he laid on the table in front of the judge. Regenvogel stared at it, his face suddenly sick and old. The badge glinted dully in the filtered sunlight coming into the saloon through the tinted, dust-streaked windows.

'What is this?' Rawley rasped. 'What are you up to, friend?'

'There you go again,' said Angel resignedly. 'I'm not your friend.'

'De . . . Department of Justice?' Regenvogel said, picking up the circular badge in trembling fingers and staring at it. The silver circle caught the sun as he showed it to Ed Fischer. Men in the row behind the Fischer boys could see the circular seal, the screaming eagle, the words *Department of Justice, United States of America.*

'That's right,' Angel said. 'Which is bad news for you, judge – if you really are a judge. Even worse if you're not.'

Fischer was turning the badge over in his hands. He

looked at Angel with a new, warier light in his eyes. Watchful, he handed the badge back to its owner.

'You could have stolen that,' he said reasonably.

'True,' Angel said. Now he opened the flat oilskin pouch he had produced at the same time as the badge, spreading out a document on the table top.

'This is my commission as a Special Investigator of the Justice Department,' Angel said, raising his voice so that everyone in the room could hear it. 'It shows that I am acting under direct orders from the Attorney-General of the United States, directly responsible through him to the President. It also says,' he said, measuring the words out carefully so that all could assimilate their meaning, 'that I can take any action which I see fit to maintain law and order, civil or military. It means I can – and do – declare this *court* about as legal as a flea-circus!'

He turned now to face the crestfallen Regenvogel, whose shuttling eyes darted from face to face seeking sympathy or support which was not forthcoming.

'Judge,' Angel said levelly. 'Stand up and tell these people what a joke this trial was, what a travesty this court was, what a mockery your sentence was. Tell them you're the sorriest specimen of a vigilante judge that ever opened Blackstone. Get on your feet, go on – *tell them*!'

There was a whiplash in his final words that made the old man jerk like a badly operated marionette, trying clumsily to get to his feet. Before Regenvogel could speak, however, Ed Fischer's urbane voice cut it. If there was a slow-burning rage behind the dark eyes, few other than Angel could see it.

'Well, *Mister* Angel,' he said softly. 'I thought there was more to you than the usual drifter. The question is: what now?'

'By the authority vested in me by the United States Government, I am placing your brother under arrest,' Angel said. 'I'll take him to Santa Fé, hand him over to the United States Marshal there. A full investigation can be made by him, and a proper trial – if a trial's needed – can be held in a United States court, with a real judge and witnesses who won't be afraid to speak the truth.'

Ed Fischer smiled, a slow wicked smile of almost boyish charm.

'Aren't you forgetting something?' he asked softly. He didn't move; but his eyes turned towards the two deputies still clutching their riot guns, to Rawley, whose sixgun was also in his hand, and to the albino at the bar. Francey King was standing watchfully tense, his weight on the balls of his feet, pale thin hands lingering lovingly near the eagle-bill butts of his twin guns. Fischer's smile widened.

'I'd say you had a tiger by the tail, Angel,' he remarked casually.

Angel shook his head sadly.

'Fischer, your brain's not connected to your mouth,' he observed. 'You plan to take on the entire United States Government?'

'Well, this little bit of it, anyway,' Fischer said easily.

'Pull the wrong string now and this country'll be so thick with law you'll smother to death,' Angel told him. 'Don't be a fool.'

Fischer threw back his head and laughed out loud. There was the faintest echo of uneasy laughter among the men watching, and Angel saw Mike Fischer lumber to his feet, his brow knitted with anger.

'Let me take him apart, Ed,' the big man said. 'I'll take that badge and jam it up his—'

Big Ed held up a hand, and his brother fell silent, as if a switch had been thrown.

'No,' Fischer said. 'He's bluffing and he knows it. Don't you Angel?'

The two men looked at each other for a long silent moment and then Fischer threw back his head and laughed again. Now Mike Fischer and Trev Rawley grinned, too. Even Regenvogel managed a watery smile.

'Nobody to back your play, Angel,' Fischer said, grinning wickedly. 'You're called, fourflusher. You're on your own!'

'Wrong, Ed!' snapped a voice. 'I'm backing him!'

Every head in the saloon turned towards the source of the words, and the crowd parted, as if on curtain rails, making a corridor at the end of which the men by the table could see the man standing by the batwing doors of the saloon. He had come in quietly, without anyone noticing, a small, compactly built man dressed in a dark suit with a neat white shirt and four-in-hand. He looked about thirty five, or roughly the same age as the heavy Sharp's .50 calibre rifle cradled easily at his hip, its long barrel casually menacing everything in front of it.

'Tell your people not to do anything stupid, Fischer!' the man snapped. 'I'm nervous enough as it is, and if anyone makes me twitch, you're going to get a bullet from this thing right through your belly!'

Fischer paled; at the thirty foot distance involved, a slug from the buffalo gun would blow a hole the size of a dinner plate through his body.

'Listen,' he said. 'Listen.'

'Tell them!' snapped the rifleman. 'Especially this freak by the bar!' Fischer's gaze scuttled to where Francey King was standing, hands tensed, itching for a try at the guns in the holsters.

'Francey,' he managed hoarsely. 'Hold off. Hold off!'

King looked towards Fischer, his lip curling, as though debating whether to try for the guns anyway, and the man at the doorway spoke again.

'He's making me nervous, Ed,' he said, not a trace of nervousness in his voice. 'I get much edgier, you're going to be spread all over that wall!'

'Francey!' Fischer shouted, just the edge of panic in his voice. King looked at Fischer with disgust, but he did as he was told. He held off, lifting his hands exaggeratedly and hooking them into his shirt at breast pocket level.

'Doc,' Rawley said, eyes never still, taking in every angle, every aspect of the situation in the saloon. 'This ain't none of your affair.' His voice was reasonable, an adult telling a child he was misguided.

'Sure,' Doc said. 'Sure. It's none of my affair if I ride like a madman to Gus Parrack's place to tend a girl who's been beaten and raped. It's none of my affair if someone shoots a sixteen-year-old Mexican kid down in cold blood. It's nobody's affair but the Fischers', right? They can do what the hell they like and it's nobody's business but theirs. Like hell! I'm making it my affair, and I'm doing it right now. And it's about time some of the spineless things that pass for people in this town did the same thing!'

There had been a murmur of surprise, tinged with anger, as he spoke. The men in the saloon were the kind who were easily swayed, and for a moment Ed Fischer felt fear for the first time. He looked towards Trev Rawley, who frowned: take it easy, the look said, we're still in control.

He was wrong.

Frank Angel turned in a surprisingly fast, unexpected movement, lifting the riot gun neatly out of the hands of the unsuspecting deputy behind him. Everyone in the saloon heard the wicked sound of the twin hammers snicking back, and there was a gasp of indrawn surprise. Rawley whirled to face Angel, but the Justice Department man wasn't even looking at him. He had jammed the barrels of the shotgun into Joe Fischer's belly, forcing the quailing youngster back, his mouth open, literally afraid to breathe. There was a cold and empty look in Angel's eyes that shocked the younger man into frozen rigidity: Angel looked as if he'd kill him just to see what he looked like dead.

'Tell your brother he's trying my patience, Joe,' Angel said softly. There wasn't an ounce of menace in his voice, but Joe Fischer's gullet jerked as he tried to swallow the ball of fear Angel's words had put there.

'Ed . . . ?' he bleated piteously, looking towards his brother.

Ed Fischer started to move forward, but Angel just looked at him and the big man stopped, spreading his hands in a placatory gesture.

'Angel, listen to me,' he said. 'Just listen.'

'Listen, hell!' Angel snapped. 'Dick, you lift the guns off

all of these sidewinders. And don't get between me or the Doc and any of them.'

'Sure thing,' Dick Webb said, moving sideways and lifting the sixguns from Ed and Mike Fischer's holsters. He held out his hand for Trev Rawley's gun. Rawley looked at him for a long second. Then he relaxed his grip and Dick Webb took the gun from his fingers.

'Don't forget our little pink friend by the bar,' Angel said. 'He looks like he might be tempted to try for those fancy guns.'

'I'd love to see him try it,' said Doc. He gestured significantly with the barrel of the Sharp's.

Now Angel took the gun away from Joe Fischer's belly and hauled him to his feet. Joe's relief at having the gun taken away from his midriff was short-lived, for no sooner was he on his feet than Angel laid the twin bores negligently against the side of Joe's neck, the barrel resting easily on his shoulder. Joe stood as if carved from stone, only his eyes moving in silent entreaty towards his older brothers.

'You were saying?' Angel asked Ed Fischer politely.

Big Ed stood for a moment, then nodded, nodded again, as if coming to some kind of reluctant decision. The growing rage behind his eyes was burning fiercely now, scarcely held in check, but held. This was not the moment and Big Ed was not a fool.

'All right,' he said. 'What do you want?'

'You know that,' Angel said.

'Yes, I suppose so,' Fischer said softly. 'You're crazy if you think you can swing it, Angel. Back off now, ride out of here. We'll give you a clear run, no strings.'

'Sure,' Angel said.

'Take the offer,' Rawley told him. 'It's the best one you'll get.'

'Sure,' Angel said again. He didn't move the gun from Joe Fischer's neck, though.

'You're going to do it the hard way, then?' Ed Fischer asked.

'Never was any other,' Angel told him.

'Then you're a fool!' Fischer burst out. 'Tell him, Rawley!'

Rawley shrugged. 'He knows,' he said. 'Don't you, Angel?'

Frank Angel nodded. He knew, all right. Right now he had the cards, the whip hand. But it was a Mexican stand-off. Fischer knew as well as he did that there was no way out. Neither of them needed it spelled out slowly. Angel might have Joe Fischer, but they had Angel. He couldn't take Joe out of Fischer's Crossing alone: that way lay outnumbered death. Equally, he could not expect to stand in town alone against the might of the Flying Fish and its riders, who could come in whenever they were ready and take Joe back. Nobody would pitch in and help man the barricades. There was Angel, the kid, and the doctor. That was all. That was what Rawley meant when he said Angel knew, and he was right. Angel knew, all right. He wasn't about to let it bother him right now.

'Move,' he told Joe Fischer.

Joe turned, stumbling, anxious not to jar the shotgun laid so carelessly upon his shoulder next to the jugular vein which everyone could see painfully throbbing in his neck.

'You too, Fischer,' Angel said to Big Ed. 'And your brother. Dick, bring Rawley and his deputies along. And you, Doc – get him on out of here!'

He jerked his chin at Francey King as he prodded Joe Fischer down the gangway between the serried rows of chairs, ignoring the gawping faces of the townspeople as Doc, with a sarcastic bow, invited Francey King to precede him through the batwing doors and out into the long shadowed afternoon sunlight.

Once outside, Angel squinted up at the sky, gauging the time. He had arrived in Fischer's Crossing about this time yesterday. It had been a hectic twenty-four hours, he reflected. Likely the next twenty four would be even fuller.

'Get on your horses,' he told the two Fischers. 'You others, too.'

Mike Fischer bayed his horse around beside his brothers, shaking his head in an almost admiring wonderment.

'You sure as hell got your gall, Angel,' he said, softly. 'It's gonna be a barrel of fun takin' you apart piece by piece.'

'I'll bet you say that to all the girls,' Angel said mirthlessly. He turned his attention to Ed Fischer. 'Get the hell out of town, Fischer. Take your tame lawmen and your freak friend with you. Show your nose within rifle range again and I'll shoot it off!'

Ed Fischer reined his horse around, his face black with anger.

'You talk a hell of a good fight, lawman,' he snapped. 'We'll see how loud you sing in due course!'

The crowd from the saloon was seeping sheepishly out of the building, sidling along the boardwalk, trying to overhear what was being said. Big Ed knew that his sovereignty had been threatened, knew his control and power had been lessened in their eyes and that now he had no choice any more. So be it: he would enjoy cropping this rooster.

'Enjoy the sunset, Mister Angel,' he said, his voice level but loud enough to be heard clearly. 'You'll never see another!'

'Jabber, jabber, jabber,' Angel said, and without warning, slashed the big man's horse across the rump with the barrel of the shotgun. The unexpected blow startled the unsuspecting animal, which screeched with pain and jumped from a standing start into a wild run, almost unseating Ed Fischer as it rocketed off down the street. For a moment, the other men watched in startled shock, and then Trev Rawley wheeled his animal around, jammed his spurs into the brute's sides, and led the others flat out into the sifting dust cloud which marked the passage of their leader.

Angel watched them go, his face reflective, the shotgun still resting negligently on Joe Fischer's shoulder.

'Frank,' Dick Webb said. 'This is Doc Day, Peter Day.'

'Doc,' Angel said. 'I want to thank you for joining the party.'

'Glad to,' Day told him. 'My pleasure, in fact.'

They were silent for a moment, watching the empty street. The dust had settled now, and they could see the small cloud of dust which marked the passage of the four Fischer men heading up the trail towards the Arabelas north of town. A brown dog meandered across the empty street.

'How many men can Fischer raise?' Angel asked aloud of nobody in particular.

'Too damned many for my liking,' Doc Day said.

'Uhuh,' Angel acknowledged, and if he saw Joe Fischer's evil smile, he didn't react. 'Time for bed, Joe,' he said, gesturing across the street towards the jail.

Joe Fischer shrugged and made no complaint as he was herded across the rutted road to the jail. A night in the *juzgado* wasn't going to kill him.

CHAPTER SIX

'Let me go in and take him,' Francey King said. 'Let me do it.'

'No,' growled Fischer.

'Ed, you know it makes more sense for me to do it. You got to let me go.' The gunman's pink eyes were bright with a special desire, and he leaned forward earnestly in his attempt to convince his employer.

'I don't "got to" do anything,' rumbled Big Ed.

They were sitting in the big old living room at the Flying Fish ranch house, Ed and his brother Mike, Trev Rawley and his deputies, Francey King, and the Flying Fish straw-boss, Don Teesdell, sprawled on the solid, simple furniture scattered around the big adobe. Old Michael J. had built the place to last, built it like a fortress up here on the northern side of the Rio Arriba where it cut a canyon through the Arabelas, which loomed beetling and dark away to the northeast, peaks frosted with perennial snow. The ranch's living room was a square, stone-floored room dominated by a huge fireplace built from native rock and surmounted by the dusty heads of animals old Michael J. had killed – grizzly, wolf, moose. The latter's magnificent antlers now had coiled ropes and old bridles hanging from them: the younger Fischers were all bachelors, and none of them had much of their father's preference for order and tidiness. Even with their slovenly life-style, however, it was a warm and cheerful room. Scattered bearskin rugs on the stone floors, brightly patterned Navajo blankets hanging on the flat-painted adobe walls softened the harsh lines. The sturdy furniture, much of it freighted in by old Michael J. for his new bride almost forty years before, had seen better days, but still glowed with the polish of hard use.

'No,' Ed Fischer said, almost as if to himself. 'This is one I aim to skin personally. And enjoy it – hear me?'

'I hear you, Ed,' Francey King said. 'But you're not thinkin' it through. Tell him, Mike.'

'Aw,' Mike Fischer said. 'He knows that, Francey. He's just mad right now, ain't you, Ed?'

He knew – they all knew – that there were often times when Big Ed wanted to go at things like a bull at a gate. By and large, they usually managed to talk it through so he saw it in a different light. He nodded to Trev Rawley and the marshal got up from his chair, uncoiling his lanky frame and standing in front of the fireplace.

'Ed, you know as well as we do that all you have to do is give the word to the boys to saddle up, ride into the Crossing, and fillet it like it was a river trout. Nobody'd get in your way, Ed – nobody'd dare! You'd haul Angel and the kid out of the jail an' string 'em up on the nearest tree without a hand bein' lifted against you. But it would be a mistake.'

'Go on,' Fischer said. 'I'm listening.'

He swilled another sizeable shot of whiskey from the bottle into the glass at his elbow, then held out the bottle to Rawley. The marshal took a small shot and set the bottle on the table. Mike Fischer looked at it longingly and licked his lips.

'This Angel,' Rawley continued. 'He's Federal law, right? You don't want to get mixed up with that, Ed. Not personally. You wipe out a Federal man and they never stop looking for why. So it's got to be kosher. Which means you're out of it. Besides, you got to think of your other interests.'

'Well,' Fischer said, as if reluctantly relinquishing the idea of personally killing Frank Angel. In actual fact, he was already a long way ahead of Rawley, had been from the start. He was just letting them think that the decision he had already made had been arrived at democratically: the first gift of the politician he planned to be. He was only too well aware that getting himself involved personally with killing a Federal officer would be a serious stumbling block to his political ambitions, and he had absolutely no intention of erecting it. He had his connections with the Ring in Santa Fé; he had certain assurances concerning a seat in the

Legislature before very long. Maybe he'd take a shot at the Governorship next term. Whatever he did, he certainly wasn't going to let one whey-faced Government snooper imperil it. Mister Angel would be taken care of.

'Well,' he said again, 'I can see your point.'

Rawley smiled. 'That's my boy, Ed,' he enthused.

'Nobody doubts we could bust them up in force,' Francey King said. 'But that would be too easy. Like taking a sledgehammer to crack a nut. We want the town to see that fixing friend Angel doesn't even make you sweat, Ed. They'll know: but they won't be able to prove a thing.'

'And you keep your hands nice and clean,' Rawley finished.

'All right,' Ed Fischer said, stifling his own triumphant smile. 'Tell me what you got in mind.'

'First, there's Angel,' Rawley said.

'Yes,' Big Ed agreed, a world of meaning in the way he said the one word.

'He's a pro, Ed,' Francey King said. 'I watched him. He's been up the trail and seen the elephant. He knows how to use guns.'

'Really?' Fischer said, letting the sarcasm come through strong.

'Let me finish,' Francey King said. 'Odds are that he's strong on guns and weak on everything else. They usually are: take my word for it.' He let an evil grin touch his bloodless lips for a moment.

'So?'

'Mike,' Francey said.

He let Ed Fischer think about that for a moment, and then saw the dawning smile on the big man's face. Big Ed nodded.

'How will you get him to bite?'

'Flag of truce,' Rawley said. 'Mike argues. Claims – very loudly – that Angel's hiding behind guns, wouldn't dare fight man to man.'

'And while he does that,' Francey King said, 'me, Eddie and Bob here will take out the kid and the doctor – if he's still with them. No—' he held up a hand to prevent Ed Fischer's automatic question. 'No, we won't kill them. Might not be too careful about how bad we hurt them, though,' he added sibilantly.

'It makes decent sense,' Rawley said. 'Nice and quiet, no killin'. But everyone in town will see it and know.'

'All right,' Fischer said. 'You break Angel. You get Joe out of jail. The kid and the doc are out of the running. What makes you think they won't wait up and try again, 'specially this Angel?'

'Cause we'll have an ace in our hole,' Rawley said. 'And we'll hang on to it until the game's finished for good.'

'All right,' Big Ed said. 'Tell me.'

Rawley told him. The others listened with dawning smiles of devilish delight on their faces as the marshal outlined his idea. It was a very simple one. And like all simple ideas, it was likeliest to work. In fact, it was so simple, Rawley said, that they had almost overlooked it, but when he had thought of it, he had suddenly realised that not only did it seal off one particularly vulnerable area of inquiry, it also meant that Dick Webb and the doctor could no more lift a hand against the Fischers than fly. Nor would they let Angel, even if he was disposed to do so after Mike Fischer had finished with him.

'I like it,' Big Ed grinned. 'It looks watertight to me. I like it.'

'Thought you would,' grinned Trev Rawley. He reached for the bottle on the table and poured drinks for all of them.

'Success!' he toasted.

'Here's to the first Angel that ever went to Hell!' Francey King replied. They all thought that was very funny indeed, and thought of quite a lot more jokes about Angels before the bottle was emptied.

There was a sort of celebration going on at the Crossing, too. The townspeople had digested the astonishing fact that Big Ed Fischer and his bravos had been faced down publicly, and that the town was freed – however temporarily

– from their domination. It was wine to their souls. The Silver King was jammed, full of men who wanted to take a drink with, shake the hands of, stand and gawp at the trio who had wrought this miracle. There was an almost boisterous, school's-out air about the place.

Billy Luskam said he was going to buy everyone a drink to celebrate what he had seen, hard though it had been to believe, earlier that day.

'Never figured to see the Fischers told to git out of the Crossing,' he chortled. 'Figured even less to *see* 'em git, tails atween their laigs! So I aim to celebrate the event while the goin's good!'

He poured himself a drink and held the glass high, rapping on the bar with a heavy bottle to attract the attention of the noisy, chattering throng in the saloon. When he had their attention, he climbed up on a stool and spoke.

'I'm proposin' a vote of thanks to Frank Angel,' he announced. Anything else he might have been going to add was lost in the yell of approval which greeted his words. The crowd eddied and swirled around Angel, who stood by the bar with Doc Day and young Dick Webb.

There was just the faintest hint of a smile on Angel's face; enthusiasm and whiskey, he thought, the one fuelling the other, had created a marvellous feeling of rebellion and power here, but it was a euphoria which would vanish the moment that Fischer and his gunmen reappeared on the skyline – leaving a vacuum of fear in its place. He felt no contempt; there were farmers in this crowd, family men, smallholders, stockmen, goatherders. They were not fighting men and their aggressiveness was not real. Most of them would never have fired a gun in anger; some would not even own one. None would understand, or appreciate, the difference between themselves and a man like Francey King until they were down with a bullet in them. The ordinary man would always hesitate a moment, a split second, the thought coming into his mind as he brought a gun into action, that when he pulled the trigger he would be killing another human being. Depending on his background and upbringing he might think about the Ten Commandments, about going to Hell; he might even think that the man he was about to kill could have a wife, children, family who would grieve for him. And while he was thinking it, the professional gunman would have shot him dead, for the pros never thought about the rights of it or the wrongs of it, or the moral necessity of it, or whether they would be forgiven by a merciful God. When a pro saw a man with a gun coming at him, he killed that man if he could. Any ponderings about right and wrong came subsequently. Which, of course, was no consolation at all to the poor bastard who was being rolled into a hole on the bare slope of the *campo santo*.

After a few minutes of being slapped on the back, urged to have a drink by complete strangers, Angel held up a hand for silence. The babble of self-congratulation died down enough for him to be heard, and he laid what he had to say to them down in a level, unemotional voice.

'I don't want to kill off your enthusiasm,' he said quietly. 'But I do want you to realise that this is a lull in the battle, not the end of the war. The Fischers aren't going to take what happened to them lying down. Ed Fischer is going to come back for his brother and if any of you gets in his way he is going to kill you.'

The men nearest to Angel shuffled their feet a little, looking uneasily at each other. At the back of the room someone fired to courage by a deeper draught than wisdom might have dictated shouted 'Let him come!'

'Yeah!' someone else chimed in. 'We'll get guns. Let him come!'

A ragged cheer greeted this pretentious boast, and those nearest Angel nodded enthusiastically to show their agreement.

'Wait on,' Angel shouted over the noise. 'You're not thinking this through. You men have wives, children. If Ed Fischer comes storming in here with all his men, loaded for bear and looking for trouble, it's not going to be any cakewalk. There'll be shooting, killing. Fischer wants me. He wants Dick here, and Doc Day. Most of all he wants his brother. He's not going to let shooting anyone stop him, is he?'

A silence followed his words. The grim reality of the picture Angel had just painted wafted a freezing chill across the alcoholic enthusiasm. There was a muttering in the crowd as the full import of what they might be getting into dawned on them.

'You staying on, Angel?' a man to one side of the bar asked.

'You better believe it,' Angel said.

'I'm staying,' Dick Webb added flatly. He pushed forward and placed himself alongside Angel at the bar. 'How about the rest of you?'

'In for a penny,' Doc Day said, pushing through the crowd.

'Thanks, Doc,' Angel said, and meant it.

'I'll back you, Angel,' Billy Luskam said from behind the bar. He reached down and lifted up his sawn-off riot gun. The bang when he slapped it on the counter made one or two of the men watching jump visibly. He looked at them with lips curled by contempt.

'What about the rest of you men?' he snapped. 'Ain't there a one of you wants to fight for his rights?'

The nearest men edged backwards, reluctant to meet the challenge in Luskam's eyes, and he watched them with deep scorn.

'Well, Jesus H. Christ,' he said, spitting on the floor. 'What kind of a town is this, anyway?'

'Hell, Billy,' one of the men in the crowd who had spoken earlier said. 'You ain't got nobody to look out for 'ceptin yourself. Some of us here has wives, kids. It's like Angel there said: we ain't fightin' men.'

'You ain't any kind of men!' Luskam began angrily, but before he could say more, Angel interrupted him.

'No use tryin' to cuss them into it, Billy,' he said quietly. 'He's right. Any of you men use a gun regular?'

There were shaken heads. One or two said 'no' aloud.

'Any of you serve in the Army, maybe?'

Again a series of negatives from the men ranged before them.

'Then you're making the right decision,' Angel told them. 'Don't be ashamed – and don't mind Billy here. He's just fightin' mad. As far as I'm concerned, anyone who can't handle a gun is more of a liability than an asset. We're going to have our hands full enough, without having to watch out for rabbits.'

'Hell, Angel,' burst out a thickset, bearded man in the front of the crowd. 'We can't expect you to face up to the Fischers without some kind of help. It's us you're protectin', dammit, an' — '

'It's my job,' Angel told them quietly. 'What I get paid for. So you people get back to your homes. Keep your families off the street. Board up your windows, lock the doors, keep your heads down. One way or the other, stay out of the way until this is all over.'

'Now see here, Angel,' one man said, coming forward out of the body of the crowd. He was a short, dark-haired man, no longer young, his face creased by the winds and suns of many summers. 'You can't just take up on behalf of all of us. Someone's got to back you up. Ain't there nothing we can do?'

'There is one thing,' Angel told him thoughtfully. 'I need a good man with a fast horse.'

'You got it,' the man said. 'I'm Bry Leavey. Run the general store.'

'Glad to know you, Leavey,' Angel said. 'Stick around. The rest of you people go on back to your homes. Do like I told you. If the Fischers string us up, you'll be better off if you've been seen not to help. If they don't . . . ' He managed a grin he didn't feel like putting on his face one tiny bit. 'It won't make no difference, anyway.'

He watched, they all watched, without expression as the crowd hesitated, breaking slowly, those in front reluctant to be seen moving away, while the others at the rear moved as unobtrusively as they could towards the batwing doors, through which they hurried out, not looking back. Then gradually the crowd was thinned, the men at the front retreated with hanging heads, not looking at the men standing by the bar. They went out shamefaced but when they reached the street their heads came up and they walked rapidly towards their homes. Angel continued to let nothing show on his face, but Billy Luskam couldn't keep in his disgust.

'Goddamn them!' he snapped. 'Lily livered sonsofbitches!'

'Leave them be,' Angel said, quietly. 'Don't blame them.'

He turned towards Luskam, putting a hand on the saloonkeeper's shoulder. 'Billy,' he said. 'I'm obliged for your support awhile back. But I'm not going to keep you to what you said. Go on, get yourself the hell out of this.'

Luskam shook his head.

'Listen Angel,' he said. 'The Fischers have been sucking my blood for years. Fifty per cent of every dollar I made in this place has gone to them all the years I been here. Fifty per cent! They've taken every damned thing except my blood. Well . . . ' He patted the riot gun lying on the polished bar, his mouth hardening with determination. 'Let's see how bad they want that!'

'All right,' Angel said. Nothing more. He was glad to have Luskam with him.

'Well,' Doc Day said, stretching his arms. 'Now what, Frank?'

'Hell,' Angel said. 'That's easy. We wait.'

CHAPTER SEVEN

They didn't have long to wait.

By the next day, the town had a curious, empty, unreal appearance sharply at odds with its normal bustle. The wide main street was deserted, the hitchrails lacking their usual half dozen or more hipshot horses standing outside the store, the saloon, the livery stable. The townspeople had taken Angel's advice, and there had been sounds of furious hammering throughout the evening, stopped now. Everyone was locked securely in his home, his shutters closed, or his windows makeshiftly boarded. Over the empty street hung an unnatural silence: no sounds of children playing in the dust, of wagons grinding up or down, of horses clopping by, no chatter of conversing housewives on the boardwalks, no clump of feet as men went about their daily business. Fischer's Crossing looked like a ghost town, and above it hung a cloud of apprehension almost visible to the naked eye.

Inside the houses scattered along the single street people waited, watched, and waited and watched, always waiting and watching the northern edge of town, the trail down from the Arabelas. That was where the Fischers would first be seen.

Angel had made his plans.

They were pretty sketchy, largely based on hunch, mostly no more than contingency plans. But the best he could do in the circumstances.

Despite Dick's most vehement protests, he had packed the youngster off with certain instructions, assuring him that his contribution might be the most valuable of all. The kid hadn't wanted to leave what he was sure would be the main arena, but Angel had convinced him that his task was dangerous and vital, and in the end Dick had gone, riding out of town with Bry Leavey and heading south across the wooden bridge. Angel had watched them go with some, but not many misgivings. He was figuring what he might do if he were Fischer, and he didn't want to leave the man any openings. There was a good chance that if Dick got everything right, he could do what he had to do. Angel hoped he was right.

After the kid and the old storekeeper had gone, he made his deployments in town. It didn't take long. Billy Luskam he stationed up on the roof of the store, with a plentiful supply of shells for his riot gun. Doc Day he placed on the roof of the jail, reached via a trapdoor in the roof of the outer office. Once on the top of the jail, Doc was surrounded by a foot-high parapet, and had a commanding view of the whole street, his field of fire almost a complete circle. With Luskam on top of the store further up the street, Angel felt reasonably confident that nothing could happen in front of the jail without one of them being able to do something about it. Doc insisted on taking his old Sharp's up on the roof with him. 'I'm used to handling it,' he told Angel. 'If I've got to hit anything, I'm a hell of a sight likelier to do it with my own gun than anything else.'

Frank Angel sensed the doctor's reluctance to consider deeply the likelihood that he would have to take human life. He knew that it must be against every tenet the man believed in, and yet he had to rely on Day being there when it counted, ready to use the gun without hesitating, for hesitation might mean Angel's own death. Without anything showing on his face he touched the man on the shoulder. He'd know soon enough, and he was a fatalist to the extent that what he had no means of changing he was ready to accept.

'What about you, Frank?' Day asked. 'What do you aim to do?'

'Me?' asked Angel, raising his eyebrows in mock surprise. 'Why I'll be right across the street on the porch of the Silver King. Just a-sittin' an' a-rockin'.'

'Whaaat?'

Angel grinned, a genuine one this time.

'No use setting a mousetrap without putting cheese in it,

Doc,' he said. 'I can keep an eye on things nicely from over there. And I'm sort of relying on you not to let the mouse eat the cheese.'

'You have any idea what they'll do, Frank?' the doctor asked.

'Not really,' Angel said. 'I'm betting they won't try a frontal attack right off. Fischer's the tricky kind. He'll want to see what he's up against. See if there's no way to do what he wants to do without unnecessary force.'

'Unnecessary force,' Doc Day smiled wryly. 'That'd be about four men, wouldn't it?'

'Aw, come on, Doc,' Angel said. 'Don't put yourself down like that. You're as good as any three Fischer riders, aren't you?'

'Sure,' Day said, holding out his hand. His fingers shook visibly. 'Nerves like steel. See? A real man of iron!'

'You'll do,' Angel said.

'I hope to hell you're right, Angel,' was the reply. 'If you're wrong, it's going to get very very lonely out there in the street.'

'It is anyway,' Frank Angel told him. 'So keep your eyes skinned. Watch the alleyways, the corners of buildings, no matter what happens on the street. Roofs, backs of buildings.'

'Got it,' Day said.

They shook hands gravely, as if sealing some kind of implicit bargain, and Angel went down the ladder. By the time Day had locked the jail door and regained his perch, Angel was already in his rocking chair on the porch of the Silver King. His feet were up on the rail, and he rocked himself gently, hat tilted forward over his eyes, looking for all the world like someone with a day to waste and nothing to waste it on, a man without a care waiting for the saloon to open so he could pour down the first dustcutter of the day.

If the town hadn't been totally deserted; if the windows of all the houses hadn't been barred and shuttered; if Day couldn't have seen Billy Luskam crouched up on the roof of the store with his riot gun ready; if the wide dusty street hadn't been completely empty except for the random scavenging chicken, Angel would have looked so ordinary that you wouldn't have even noticed he was there.

As it was, he stuck out like a black widow spider on a whitewashed wall.

Mike Fischer grinned like a wolf.

He kneed his horse into motion, cantering down the bluff and back on to the trail, moving into the fringes of town, down the main street. He hardly saw the place, the shacks, adobes, dugouts. If he noticed that the windows were boarded up, he didn't show it. If he saw the slight movements that revealed people were watching from behind them, he didn't show that either. He rode easily down the centre of the street, the big store on his left, coming up to the Silver King with the makeshift flag of truce – a square of linen torn from one of the bedsheets up at the ranch – with a confident smile on his face. He saw Angel on the porch of the saloon. Angel sat gently rocking in the chair, his eyes wary.

'Angel!' Mike Fischer shouted, loud enough so that people would be able to hear. 'Come on out where I can see you!'

'You can see me,' Angel said levelly. 'And I can see your flag of truce. What do you want?'

'I come into town without no gun, Angel,' Mike Fischer said. 'To see if you're any kind of a man at all.'

'The connexion escapes me, but I'm sure you'll explain,' Angel said.

'Us Fischers don't want no gun trouble, not in our own town,' Fischer shouted. 'We don't want none of our people hurt.'

'Good enough,' Angel said. 'Ride out and there won't be any trouble.'

Mike Fischer threw back his head, a gigantic bellow of forced laughter exploding from him.

'Hear him?' he shouted aloud. His voice bounced off the

empty walls, echoed slightly. 'You skulkin' diaper-changers? Your guardian Angel don't want no trouble!'

He slid off the back of the pony and slapped it across the rump, sending the animal skittering away until it was halted, ground-hitched, by the trailing reins. He tossed the makeshift flag of truce aside with a sweep of his arm.

'Now hear *me*!' he shouted, turning his head towards the blank windows and closed shutters. 'Hear what the Fischers want! I'm goin' to take your little Angel apart with my bare hands, but afore I do it, every one of you take notice – I got no gun. No knife. Nothin' but bare hands. Us Fischers don't think your Angel's even worth wastin' a bullet on. Now, o' course, he can shoot me down if I go after him. But that'll be cold murder, and I don't figger your Angel can pull that!' He whirled now, his shoulders hunching, forehead creasing into a belligerent scowl as he faced Angel, who was rising from the rocking chair and stepping down into the street.

'All right, Angel!' he shouted, flexing his huge paws. 'Fight or die, you motherfucker!'

Francey King and the two deputies, Eddy Lamb and Bob Wight, had sifted along the dried-out bed of the Rio Arriba, moving downstream until they were beneath the bridge by the time that Mike Fischer pushed his horse into movement on the bluff at the northern edge of town. Now they moved, crouched low, through the coarse scrub growing on the open ground between the river bank and the rear of the houses on the street. The riot of thorn and twisted sagebrush was almost chest high, and tangled densely to within twenty or thirty feet of the southern side of the jail building. Their timing was almost perfect – they made their run for the rear door of the jail in exactly the same moment that Mike Fischer, a hard, excited light in his squinting eyes, lurched into movement, his paws reaching out for Frank Angel.

Frank Angel stood, his weight neatly poised on the balls of

his feet, ready for Mike Fischer's bull-like charge. When he saw the flicker of movement in the open space to the left and rear of the jail, he made a split-second decision that cost Mike Fischer his life. Angel had been prepared, preparing, to handle Mike Fischer the way that he had been taught to handle any man who physically outmatched him. The rule the Justice Department taught was: *survive*. Fair play had little to do with it. He would have simply buffaloed the big man and dragged him into the jail; but that was before he saw the men moving to attack the jail which Doc Day was holding alone and he knew he could take no chance, no chance at all, with Mike Fischer. Into his mind's eye came the picture of the featureless gymnasium in the draughty old building on Pennsylvania Avenue in Washington, the little man watching him, the slanting eyes wary, the carefully-held hands always moving, constantly weaving. Kee Lai, the Korean, had taught him that there was a force, which was called *ch'i*, which he must learn to summon and control at will. It was the sum of the whole man, everything, his essence, brought instantly to one place for one moment and then used, without mercy.

So he stood now with his hands held in a certain way, swaying lightly on the balls of his feet, perfectly balanced as Mike Fischer came at him like a Miura from the *toril*. The big man's rush was blind and quite without science, brute strength without brain. Angel let Fischer get within reach and then he hit him once with his right hand. The first three fingers were folded so that the central knuckles protruded and the little finger was folded away beneath them. His hand moved no more than six inches but it stopped Mike Fischer as if he had run into a steel door. Even as he coughed blood from his shattered larynx, his huge frame paralysed by the shocking blow which had cut off his air supply, Angel's left hand, held almost exactly as was his right, came up and into a half circle. It drove with terrible accuracy into the soft spot directly to the right and just below the ribcage, rupturing Mike Fischer's diaphragm as if it had been wet tissue paper. The man lurched over, his body folding down, and Angel could have let him fall, to writhe in agony on the dusty street until he died. No doctor could have done anything to save Mike Fischer: he had been effectively dead from the moment Angel had made his decision three seconds earlier. Now as the big man's head came down, Angel hit Mike Fischer for the third time.

There are seven very delicate vertebrae at the base of the skull. The weakest point in this chain is the place where the seventh vertebrae meets and joins the eighth, which in turn is part of the rigid bone structure of the shoulders. All of Angel's strength, all of his weight, and all of the long and careful training he had been given were behind the awful chopping blow which he delivered with the hardened edge of his right hand precisely to that place. It broke Mike Fischer's spine with a sound almost exactly like the one that is made when a dead branch is snapped off a tree and the big man was quite dead when he hit the ground face down.

Even as Mike Fischer's body drove into the ground and fluffed up a small cloud of dust, Frank Angel was in motion, knowing without even having to glance at the man's body that Fischer was dead, that nothing human could have survived the things he had done.

Francey King and his two men were still no more than halfway across the clearing between the edge of the brush and the rear of the jail when Angel's gun came up, his first shot tearing a wicked furrow through the upper thigh of the thickset deputy, Lamb, whacking the man off his feet in a welter of arms and legs with a mewling screech of agony, bright blood staining the ground.

King whirled, astonished, eyes widening at the sight of Angel moving forward in a fast running crouch, the curiously flattened body of Mike Fischer inert in the dusty street behind him. The gunman was very good, and he reacted fast to the realisation that it had taken Angel less than five seconds to dispose of the big man, whirling cat-like for the shelter of the jail wall as he saw Angel go down in the middle of the street on one knee, the sixgun resting across his own left forearm, sighting deliberately. King grinned with satanic triumph, knowing as he moved that he would be faster than Angel, more accurate. His two .38s would outgun Angel, who was isolated and without cover. He screeched at Bob Wight to come around over to the right to distract Angel. Wight got up and started to run and Francey King flipped up his .38s, pink eyes wild red with raging calm. He saw Angel's face clear and clean and then there was an awful black snap as if the world had come off its hinges and he could taste dirt in his mouth and then nothing.

Angel's carefully aimed shot lifted Bob Wight up off the ground and tossed the man backwards like a discarded coat, the rising bullet arcing through his body and tearing his heart to pieces. In exactly the same moment Doc Day's Sharp's .50 belched fire, its terrible whanging slam from the roof of the jail flattening all the other sounds, the heavy slug smashing down into the back of Francey King's neck at an acute angle and then blowing away the front of the gunman's body, killing him almost instantly. Francey King never even knew who had shot him down.

Now Eddy Lamb came scrambling out from behind the jail, where he had rolled into a shallow runoff. His clothes were covered in dust and blood and his eyes were wide with panic and pain. He emptied the gun in his hand wildly, as if the bullets might erect some shield between him and the awful scything death which had claimed his comrades in what seemed like only the space of several heartbeats. He quartered away around the rear of the jail, and then staggered out into the street, lurching towards the store, his eyes bulging and his only conscious thought to try to get somewhere where he could not be killed. But his wounded leg wouldn't carry him and he sank to the ground, crying like a child, as Billy Luskam came scrambling out of the doorway of the store and stood over him with his riot gun trained on the cringing figure.

Angel went over there and kicked the sixgun out of Lamb's nerveless fingers, holstering his own gun at the same time. Smoke and dust drifted in a sliding veil across a patch of sunlight and then became invisible in the darker shadows next to it.

It was all over.

The man on the ground groaned and tried to sit up, waves of pain washing the colour from his face. He turned pleading eyes up towards Frank Angel, but whatever he saw on Angel's face was enough to make him shield his own as if he feared being struck.

'Get up, if you can!' Angel told him, harshly.

'Oh, God, please, don't, please, God, Angel, don't, please. . . . ' Lamb babbled.

Luskam and Angel ignored him, watching as Doc Day poked his head outside the jail door, looked right and left up and down the street, and then came out. He ran across to where the others stood.

'Great God in Heaven, Angel,' he said. 'Did you . . . did we?'

He gestured towards the sprawled figures in the street.

'It's all over,' Angel said. 'For the moment, anyway.'

'Sweet angels of mercy,' Day said. 'What did you hit Fischer with?'

'No matter,' was the harsh reply. 'He's just as dead.'

Day looked up, sharply, seeing something in the other's eyes that he had not expected, a sort of regret, a hint, an indication that Angel felt that he had killed Mike Fischer without hesitation or qualm, but with regret – the regret of a man who knows that he will not fail, no matter what the other does.

'What about this one, Frank?' Billy Luskam wanted to know. 'We throw him in with Joe?'

Eddy Lamb's eyes shuttled anxiously from Angel's face to Day's, from Day's to Billy Luskam's, and then back to Angel's. When the latter turned to look down at him, Lamb cringed, tense with fear.

'This is twice you've crossed my path,' Angel said to him softly. 'Once as Rawley's deputy, once now.'

'Listen, Mister Angel . . . ' Lamb began, haltingly.

'Listen nothing!' Angel snapped. 'You're lucky they're

not taking you out of here in a bag of sand. Cross my tracks a third time and they will. Hear me?'

'I hear you,' Eddy Lamb said. 'I hear you.'

'Right,' Angel said. 'Now you get on your horse and go tell Ed Fischer what happened down here. Tell him his brother and his freak killer are dead, and then keep riding. If I ever see your face again, I'll shoot it off. Savvy?'

'You bet,' Lamb said, anxiously getting up, helped by Day and the saloonkeeper. 'You bet, Angel. Don't you worry. I'll git. You'll never see me again, don't you worry.'

'Don't you worry about me worrying,' Angel told him. 'Get the hell out!'

Eddy Lamb nodded, and after Billy Luskam came back with a horse, climbed into the saddle, his face creased with pain.

'Thanks for catchin' up my horse, Billy,' he said.

'Don't thank me,' Luskam told him sourly. 'Thank God you're alive to ride it!'

Without another word he slapped the horse across the rump, and the animal whirled around, moving off up the street at a canter, Eddy Lamb reeling in the saddle until he got control of the horse and they disappeared in their own dust at the northern edge of the town.

Angel took a deep breath; he let the tension run out of him like tapwater. Then he walked across the street to where Francey King lay in the dirt. The flies were busy and he turned away.

Doc Day was stooping over the body of Mike Fischer. He got up shaking his head, but if there was anything he wanted to say, he managed not to say it.

'They had it set up real neat,' Billy Luskam said.

'But not neat enough,' Angel replied. 'They figured on Mike giving them enough time for what they wanted to do.'

'It sure as hell was hectic while it lasted,' Doc said.

'That it was,' Frank Angel agreed. 'You did fine, just fine.'

'Well . . . ' Luskam wanted to know. 'What happens now, Frank?'

'You run a saloon,' Angel said with a slow grin. 'Suggest something.'

Billy Luskam looked at him for a moment, then grinned too.

'Got you,' he said. 'That's a hell of a good idea. Doc?'

'Don't mind if I do,' Day said. 'Purely medicinal, you understand.'

'Of course, of course,' Luskam said. 'What else?'

They went into the deserted saloon together, knowing that their humour was forced, to keep away the spectres of the men they had killed and the way they had killed them. The bodies of the dead men lay in the street where they had fallen and none of the three looked back. After a long while, one or two of the townspeople came out of their houses and stood in the street, talking very quietly. One or two of them looked northeast where the thunderheads were piling up over the Arabelas, and their faces were troubled. Angel had laid down his challenge brutally, violently, unequivocally. The die was cast. From now on it would be a fight to the death.

CHAPTER EIGHT

Frank Angel guessed right.

Trev Rawley took the Flying Fish straw-boss Don Teesdell with him and left the Fischer spread about the same time that Francey King and Mike Fischer larruped their horses south down the trail towards the Crossing. Unlike them, Rawley and his sidekick pushed their horses up Arabela canyon until they reached the old mountain trail that led through a ragged gap in the mountains and down into the canyon of the Rio Abajo. It wasn't long until the two men were looking down on the cottonwood-shaded hollow where the Flying W. ranchhouse lay, L-shaped and compact, the neat adobe building apparently deserted. Rawley pulled his horse to a stop on a brush-stippled bluff overlooking the place, scanning the surrounding area and the corral off to one side of the main ranch building.

He nodded with satisfaction.

'Just the girl, by the look of it,' he said to Teesdell. 'An' the Mex woman, probably.'

Teesdell shook his head, pointing downhill towards the river.

'Aha,' Rawley said. The Mexican woman, Deluvina Martinez, was slapping washing against a flat stone to get the water out of them. The rolling stream was whitened with the lye soap suds.

'All right,' Rawley said. 'Let's move.'

They tied the horses up in a brush stand maybe a hundred yards upstream from where Deluvina was, moving on silent feet through the long grass and brush skirting the river until they were very close to her. She was singing to herself as she did the washing, a tuneless song that ceased abruptly as a twig snapped under Trev Rawley's spurred boot. Deluvina turned like a startled animal, poised to flee, but the marshal was already on her, his big hand clamping across her mouth to prevent the scream, other arm clamping Deluvina's arms so that she could do little more than struggle ineffectually. Rawley lifted her off her feet and whirled her around, her back to a big boulder on the edge of the river.

Deluvina Martinez closed her eyes as if in pain. She was not a young woman, and she seemed stunned and very frightened by this sudden assault. When she opened her eyes again she saw the knife in Trev Rawley's hand and now real fear showed on her face. Her eyes rolled up and she looked as if she might faint.

'Don't you even squeak, *señora*,' Trev Rawley hissed to her. '*Comprende?*'

Deluvina nodded her head anxiously, eyes shuttling from Rawley to Teesdell and back again. She was trembling like a leaf, now.

'Where's the girl?' Rawley asked her. '*A donde es la señorita?*'

'*Casa*,' the woman managed. '*En la casa*.'

'In the house, eh?' Rawley nodded. 'Alone? *Solo?*'

'*Si, solo*,' Deluvina managed.

Rawley released her, and the woman slumped back against the big rock, relief and anxiety fighting in her expression.

'Stay here!' Rawley told her, pointing at the ground. '*Aqui! Comprende?*'

'*Aqui, si*,' she whispered, nodding to show she understood.

She watched with wide, expressionless eyes as they moved away and ran quickly through the shading oak and willow to the edge of the open space in front of the ranch house. Rawley held up an arm and Teesdell skidded to a stop behind him.

'What?' he said.

'Take it easy,' Rawley said. 'Don't want to flush our little bird out too early.'

They crossed the yard fast on soft feet, coming to the wall of the house next to the door, turning backs to, edging to the doorway and Rawley nodded. Teesdell nodded back, okay, and Rawley went in fast through the open door, the hallway dark and cool.

There were doors on both sides of the hall, the one at the

far end standing ajar. They could hear the light sound of a woman's voice humming tunelessly, the kind of song a woman sings when she is brushing her hair before a party she knows she will enjoy. Teesdell touched Rawley's shoulder, pointing ahead with his chin, and Rawley nodded again, moving forward with the sixgun in his hand towards the open doorway.

As they did so the first door on the left hand side of the hallway opened and Dick Webb stepped into the hall behind them, his father's shotgun cocked and ready in his hands.

Rawley felt, rather than saw, the movement behind him and whirled on cat feet, the sixgun coming up. Teesdell turned, startled, in the same moment, his face going as slack with shock as Rawley's. Their eyes fixed on the gaping bores of the old shotgun, looking as big as cave entrances; and as they did Susie Webb came out of the bedroom behind them with a sixgun in her hand. It looked almost too big for her to handle, but there was grim determination in the set of her mouth, and she held the big gun steady with both hands, fully cocked, its barrel not more than six inches from the centre of Rawley's spine.

They were cold-cocked and they knew it.

Rawley shrugged and let the sixgun slide out of his hand. It hit the carpet covering the boarded floor with a dull clunk as the marshal pasted a weak grin on to his face.

'You, too,' Dick Webb said to Teesdell, gesturing with the shotgun.

Rawley looked at him for a long moment, then back over his shoulder at the girl. She gestured with the sixgun and a nervous tic flickered in the marshal's cheek.

'Do it!' he snapped, harshly.

'Wait on,' Teesdell said, softly. There was a strange look on his face.

'The gun, Teesdell,' Dick Webb said. 'Don't have me tell you again.'

'That thing loaded, kid?' Teesdell asked. 'Really loaded? For bear?'

'You're about to find out the hard way,' Dick Webb gritted, as Teesdell took a soft, tentative step forward. The twin barrels came up, and Teesdell raised his hands palm out, shoulder high, a small smile still on his face.

'Easy, kid,' he said.

'Stand still and shuck your gun, then!' Dick Webb snapped.

'Sure,' Teesdell said softly. He took another small, sibilant step. Rawley watched, utterly still, gaze shuttling from the straw-boss to Dick Webb and back. Teesdell took another step.

'You going to blast me down, kid?' he whispered. 'Right here in front of your little sister?'

'Don't make me,' Dick Webb warned. But he took a half step backwards.

'I don't think you could do it, Dickie,' Teesdell said. His voice was almost fatherly, even if there were small beads of sweat on his forehead and upper lip. He took another small step, almost within arm's length of the end of the gun barrels now. 'Not in cold blood,' he added. 'Murder me, I mean.'

'Get back now, Teesdell,' Dick Webb said, and there was just the faintest edge of a hint of unease in his young voice now. Rawley heard it and hope blossomed inside him. Teesdell heard it and grinned.

'You better give me the gun, Dickie,' he said softly. 'Afore there's an accident.'

'Keep back!' Dick shouted, and as he did Don Teesdell reached up and grabbed the barrels of the shotgun, forcing them aside to point at the wall, twisting the weapon around so that Dick couldn't pull the triggers as Trev Rawley spun around, hands reaching for the girl behind him. He fell back screeching with astonished pain because in that moment Susie Webb yanked on the trigger of the sixgun in her hand.

The lancing flame from the barrel seared across Rawley's ribs, dragging a shout of agony from him as the heavy bullet whacked into Don Teesdell's back. It smashed him face forward against the adobe wall of the hallway, his fingers hooked like claws trying to keep him upright, a twisted rictus of pure agony on his face. The heavy bullet had shattered his spine and he went down the wall like a wounded cat, dead before he collapsed on the floor, before the eddying black smoke had swirled out of the confines of the hallway. Trev Rawley looked down at the body of the dead straw-boss, his expression one of shocked astonishment.

'You . . . killed him,' he said.

'That's right,' Susie Webb replied. Then she turned and ran into the bedroom and left Dick Webb alone there with the shotgun pointed unwaveringly at Rawley's belly. Rawley offered no sign of resistance; he stared down at Teesdell's body as though it could tell him something.

'It was a set-up,' he said, as though to himself.

Dick Webb said nothing. Rawley's head came up and there was anger in his eyes now, anger at having been taken like a fool.

'You set us up,' he said.

'That's right, Rawley,' Dick Webb told him. 'You were set up.'

'God damn you, it won't do you any good,' the marshal cursed. 'By the time I got here, your friend Angel was already dead.'

'I wouldn't bet on it, Rawley,' Dick Webb said. 'But there's an easy way to find out. Let's go.'

'Go?' Rawley asked. 'Where?'

'Back to the Crossing,' Dick Webb said.

'You're taking me back to the Crossing?' Rawley said. He looked at Dick Webb as if the youngster had gone mad. 'Ed Fischer will hang you when we get there!'

'Don't bet on that, either,' Dick Webb said.

'Get my horse and we'll soon see,' Rawley said.

'That we will,' Dick Webb replied. 'How does it feel to be the ace-in-the-hole, Rawley? Instead of holding it?'

'I don't get you.'

'Then you're dumber than I gave you credit for,' Dick Webb said shortly. 'I'm going to ride you into the Crossing,

Rawley. If Angel is okay, you'll be okay, too. You'll just go into the *juzgado* to wait for the U.S. Marshal to get here. But if Angel has been killed, I'm going to shoot you stone dead in full view of the whole town.'

'You're plumb loco,' Rawley said. 'You've lost your marbles!'

'Maybe so, maybe not,' the younger man said. 'Either way, Rawley, it's going to be your bad luck. Feeling in good shape?'

'Good shape? What the hell does that mean?'

'You got a long walk ahead of you.'

'Walk?'

'That's right, Rawley,' Dick Webb told him grimly. 'It's around ten miles, give or take a furlong, over to the Crossing.'

'*Walk*? To the Crossing?'

Trev Rawley's face was a study in horrified realisation of what Dick Webb was going to do to him. He was a horseman, a Westerner, a man who would climb on to his pony to cross a street rather than walk the ten yards. Walking was for farmers, cowherds, sheepmen. He looked at his beautifully tooled leather boots with their high heels. In a saddle, they were the most practical footwear ever invented. On the ground they were as useful as an Iron Maiden, and after ten miles, a man's feet would be as sorry a mess as what a roadrunner would leave of a sidewinder.

'You . . . you wouldn't make a man walk that far?' Rawley said. He tried not to make it sound like he was begging, because his pride was too strong for that. It came out like he was begging anyway.

'Not a man,' Dick Webb said, emphasising the noun. 'However, that's a breed you and your kind don't qualify for. Let's go, Rawley!'

The marshal stood silent for a moment and then he began to swear. He started slowly, working himself up to a crescendo, letting loose every filthy word he had ever heard and inventing some along the way, calling Dick Webb and Frank Angel every vile thing he could put tongue to. Dick

Webb stood impassively until Rawley started to run out of breath, and then he shook his head sadly, teacher with wayward child.

'Tut, tut, Rawley,' he said wearily. 'Don't you know there are ladies about?' He laid the barrel of the shotgun alongside Rawley's head, smacking the man hard enough to make him reel but not so hard that he went down unconscious. Rawley shook his head like a dog coming out of a river, senses stunned by the sudden blow. The flow of curses was cut off like a turned tap.

'There,' Dick Webb said, mock-soothingly. 'That's better. Susie, you about ready?' he shouted.

'Ready,' came the girl's voice from outside.

Dick Webb poked Rawley into movement with the barrel of the shotgun and the marshal stumbled outside into the bright sunlight. There was a buckboard at the door, and Rawley saw that the Mexican woman Dulvina was sitting in the back, satisfaction at his plight written plain on her broad, beaming face. Rawley looked at the man holding the reins.

'Parrack!' he exclaimed. 'What are you doing here?'

'Doin' what I ought to've done years back, Rawley,' the grizzled rancher snapped. 'Fightin' back against you and your treacherous kind!'

'By God,' Rawley swore, 'you're brave enough when there's no danger!'

'Might say the same of you, marshal,' Parrack said unabashed. 'Leastways you never seen me tryin' to make war on young girls.'

Now Susie Webb came around the side of the house leading a pony. She came around by her brother, touching his arm. He took the looped lariat from her, and then watched as she climbed up into the buckboard with Parrack. Then Dick Webb climbed aboard the cowpony and lightly tossed the loop of the lariat, the other end of which was snugly tied to the pommel of his saddle, around Trev Rawley's neck, pulling it firmly tight.

'All set,' he said, looking around. 'Let's go. And Rawley –

don't you make too hot a pace, y'hear? This pony can't do much better than around twenty miles to the hour.'

Trev Rawley opened his mouth to curse his captor, but as he did Dick Webb yanked on his end of the rope and the noose tightened mercilessly, making Rawley's eyes bulge as his wind was cut off. He clawed at the noose with his fingers, while Dick Webb shook the rope and it loosened.

'You watch your mouth, Rawley,' he advised. 'Or you're gonna get all choked up about things.'

He turned his attention to his sister.

'Susie, you get moving now. Take good care of them, Gus. You know what to do?'

'Bet your ass!' was Parrack's reply. 'Beggin' your pardon, ma'am!'

'Don't worry, Dick,' Susie said. 'We'll get there.'

He nodded and smiled, looking down at her. The bruises and scratches on her face were still raw and angry, but there was clear determination in her eyes and he knew that physically, at least, she would be fine. The rest, he imagined, would take time and nothing else could help.

'*Vaya con Dios,*' he said softly.

'*Con Dios,*' she replied, as Gus Parrack slapped the reins across the back of the team and they rattled off out of the yard, going upstream towards the ford just northeast of the ranch. From there they could cut across to the road running due south from the Arabelas towards Fort Union.

'Well, Rawley,' he said, switching his attention to the marshal, who was watching the receding dustcloud with frowning intensity. '*Vamonos*!'

'Where are they going?' Rawley asked, jerking his head towards the direction the buckboard had taken.

'I'll give you one guess,' Dick Webb said, with a grin.

Trev Rawley passed up the offer. South and a little westward, not more than seventy miles away, lay Fort Union. It didn't take a genius to figure that Angel would send for help from there and that Susie Webb, the Mexican woman, and Gus Parrack would make powerful representatives. Time was running out, unless Ed's boys had already taken care of Angel at the Crossing. If they hadn't. . . . He started walking, his mind racing furiously. Dick Webb rode easy in the saddle behind him, shotgun cradled. There was no trace of pity on his face for the stumbling, dust-coated figure in front of him. For all the bantering air he had put on, Dick Webb was not going to forget why Trev Rawley had come to the Flying W., nor let him off the hook for doing it. He wondered if Angel and the Doc were in good shape. There was no way to be absolutely sure, but he was confident. Angel was that kind of man: he gave you confidence. He looked at Trev Rawley. The marshal was stumbling along, head down, every line of his frame rigid with determination. His mind, although there was no way Dick Webb could know it, was seething with plans for revenge, for Rawley was as confident as Dick Webb that when they reached the Crossing, Angel would be dead and he delivered. He ploughed on, thinking of what he would do when he had a gun in his hand again.

CHAPTER NINE

Finally, Big Ed Fischer was in a cold, empty, killing rage.

He sat now in the big armchair in the empty living room of the big ranch, letting it build, build, stoking, nursing it by going over and over and over the things that had happened in the last twenty four hours.

At first it had been an uncontainable rage mixed with shame which had found an outlet in physically kicking out of the house the blubbering cretin who had brought him the news of how Angel had killed Mike Fischer and Francey King in the empty street of the Crossing. The man had made it sound as if Angel had placed a dozen guns on the rooftops, and that there had been no chance for them to do what they had gone into the town to do. For Mike, his brother, Big Ed felt no grief. Mike had never been bright, never really much use to Ed in his ambitions. What he felt was shame: shame that the crawling morons who infested the shanty to which his father had given a name should now see that name humbled in the dust of its street. Rage and shame possessed him, but they did not as yet fire him to stupidity: Ed Fischer was many things, but he was not a fool.

He sat and considered Angel. The man was patently not to be underestimated: somehow or other he had killed Mike, he had killed Francey King. The garbled chattering of a demented second-rater gave Ed Fischer very little to go on in the way of evidence as to how Angel had done it, but in the ultimate analysis that didn't matter. He had done it, and therefore some other way had to be found to take him.

What if some stupid farm kid, with notions of chivalry probably culled from Walter Scott, took it into his head to start trouble in the Crossing? That could be handled. What if, on top of that, ill-luck brought a wandering representative of the Department of Justice into the town? That could be handled, too: he wouldn't be the first of his breed to disappear without trace out in the vastness of the West. It was the combination which was wrong, the twin chanceness of Angel alive and Joe in jail that he saw looming as threat to his ambitions, to the opening of the first doors into the Legislature. But he would not compound those chances into a major blow by acting rashly, although his body and mind seethed with racing red anger and the desire to exact vengeance publicly before every snivelling cur in the town. That would come, he told himself, sitting back in the big chair and banking the fires of his rage. That would come when Rawley got back with the Webb girl.

So Francey King had been wrong in supposing he could take Angel by surprise. That was no great loss. There were plenty more guns for hire. He had almost a dozen men ready to ride whenever he gave the word.

But Francey's other idea: to kidnap the girl, use her as exchange bait, a swap for Joe – that idea had had a simple, sledgehammer effectiveness that Fischer had liked. No devious scheming, no tortuous planning which could break down because of ineptitude on the part of the men sent to carry it out. One bold stroke – he rolled the phrase around in his mind, liking it, planning to commit it to memory for use on other occasions. One bold stroke. The girl was only a pawn, and like all girls she'd come around once the thing was over. She'd see the light, marry Joe, and then the Webb place would become a part of the Flying Fish, the biggest spread outside of Chisum's and the Spanish grant ranches in the Territory. The girl ought to jump at the chance of marriage to the brother of a future Governor, he told himself, not really believing it, not really caring whether he believed himself or not – just calming his own anger, honing it and refining it down until it was a rapier and not a club. Anger was a stupid failing, and angry men made stupid mistakes.

So Ed Fischer poured himself some more whiskey, lit himself another of his fat cigars, and watched the clock crawl across the hours until he could wait no longer, and sent three of his riders out to look for Rawley. They came back with the news that finally drove Ed Fischer into his cold, empty, uncontrollable rage.

The Webb ranch had been locked and shuttered, deserted. In the bushes near the river they had found Rawley's chestnut and Don Teesdell's bay, but no sign at first of either man. After a careful search, they found Teesdell lying dead in the barn, shot in the back at close range. Nothing else, except a set of tracks that made no sense. One rider and a man on foot had set out west along the trail towards the Crossing. A buckboard had gone the other way, most likely heading for the Fort Union road. They had followed the tracks of the horseman and the man on foot, puzzled by them, but had not caught up before they reached the point in the trail where it forked north towards the Flying Fish.

It was grossly unfair of him to expect ordinary riders to work out what had happened at the Flying W., and Ed Fischer knew it, but he ranted at them for twenty minutes just the same, working himself to a peek of anger as he cursed their dumb stupidity, damned their obtuseness, and spat upon their lack of enterprise and imagination. Didn't they have eyes to see? Brains to think with?

The men stood with their heads bowed like cattle waiting for a storm to pass. They knew better than to enter any demurrer when the Boss was in this mood.

Finally, the tirade was over and they were dismissed. They trooped out with sullen faces while Big Ed hurled himself into the easy chair, clamping his teeth on his cigar as if it were a live thing. He sloshed more whiskey into his glass, pouring it down his throat as if it were water, mind turning over what he conjectured to have happened.

Somehow Angel had anticipated his every move.

Rawley and Teesdell, instead of taking the girl, had been deadfalled, tricked. Teesdell was dead, which meant they were keeping Rawley for something else. Angel would want witnesses, of course. Who better than Rawley, who knew more of Ed Fischer's activities than any other man? The buckboard going towards the Fort Union road meant only one thing. Someone – the girl, more than likely – was presently on the way to the Fort for help, no doubt carrying word from the Justice Department man. And much too far ahead for anyone to be able to catch up with her.

How long did he have – today, tonight, tomorrow? Not much more than that. He shook his head like a taunted bull. Francey King gone, Mike gone, Teesdell gone – some of his best men. With Rawley in Angel's hands, Joe in jail, there was only himself left. All this in so short a time! All this because of one man! He spoke the name.

'Angel!' he said. It was a curse, a threat, a promise. 'Angel!'

He rose to his feet and shook his fist at the sky he could see through the grimy, dustcoated windows. 'Angel!' he shouted. 'God damn your soul to Hell!'

Dickie Boyd, a rider who'd been with the Flying Fish spread since the days when old Michael J. was alive, came running into the house, gun in hand, drawn by the shouts of inarticulate rage, and found Big Ed smashing his fist against the rough adobe wall, his knuckles torn and bleeding, mouthing the name of the Justice Department man over and over and over again. Big Ed's eyes were empty, lit only by madness. His brain was possessed by a blind, cold empty killing rage and when Boyd laid a hand on his arm, Big Ed shook it off as though it were a bothersome insect.

'Ed!' snapped Boyd. 'Ed, for Christ's sake, what is it?'

'Angel!' Fischer sobbed. 'Angel!'

'Ed!' Boyd tried again. 'Get a hold of yourself, Ed!'

Fischer turned, facing the older man with wild, staring eyes, his whole body shaking now with the strength of his anger.

'Get every man on the place into the saddle!' he shouted. 'Every man armed! Rifles, anything you can lay your hands on!'

'Listen to me, Ed!' Boyd shouted back. 'Wait. You're not thinkin' straight—'

'Do what I tell you!' thundered Ed Fischer, and Dick Boyd quailed at the rage in the man's voice. 'Do what I say!'

'All right, Ed,' Boyd said, edging back away from the big man. 'All right. Take it easy!'

'Easy, is it?' Fischer growled. He was getting himself under control, the madness was going out of his eyes, and Dick Boyd breathed a silent sigh of relief. 'I'll show you what easy is, bucko! We're going down to the Crossing and we're going now. Once and for all, I'm going to put an end to that Justice Department sonofabitch!'

'Ed—' Boyd tried for the last time.

'Move, damn you!' Fischer whirled on him.

Boyd argued no more. He knew better than to try to reason with Big Ed when rage possessed him like this. He ran out into the yard shouting orders, and riders tumbled out of the bunkhouse towards their gear. Within a few minutes the place was a milling hive of activity, men saddling horses, checking weapons, stuffing ammunition into saddlebags or pockets.

Twenty minutes later, Ed Fischer came out of the ranch house to where they waited expectantly in a half-circle, not speaking. Miraculously – or so it seemed to his riders – Big Ed had clamped down a lid on the seething cauldron of his rage. He was just cold killing mad. They moved out behind him on to the trail leading down the canyon, silent as ghosts and deadly as the plague.

'Sweet angels of mercy!' Doc Day shouted. 'Will you look at *that*?'

That was Dick Webb riding across the wooden bridge at the southern end of town, coming up the centre of the wide, empty street with Trev Rawley stumbling ahead of him at the end of a rope. As if by magic, faces appeared at windows, doors opened, to see the incredible sight of the town marshal being brought in like some renegade Apache. Rawley's clothes were covered in thick layers of dust that had caked and been turned to runnels of mud on his face by either tears of rage or streams of sweat. His fine soft leather boots were in tattered ruin, and he was limping heavily on the right leg. His hair was matted, his eyes as wild as those of a captive beast; and when he saw the people coming out on to the street to watch his ignominy, a steady stream of croaking sounds that might have been curses stuttered from his broken lips. He cursed the people for seeing him like this, and he cursed whatever gods he believed in because the fact that they were there, the fact that nothing happened, meant that Angel was still in control of the Crossing. So he stumbled on, head swinging from side to side. The boy rode behind him on the horse, head up, as if he was leading a circus into town. Dick Webb had a shotgun cradled across his forearms and he looked as proud as a new lieutenant on his first patrol.

Angel got to his feet on the porch of the Silver King as he heard Doc Day's shout. He could see Billy Luskam scrambling to get down from the roof of the store, wanting to see this spectacle at closer range, and shouted to the saloonkeeper to stay where he was. Billy either didn't hear or didn't want to, and kept on coming; and it was precisely the moment that he came out into the street that Big Ed Fischer led his riders into the northern end of the street at a flat, attacking run.

Just like that they were suddenly in full view, and the men and women who had come out to see Trev Rawley being led through the street scattered off the boardwalks like startled blackbirds. Rawley looked up and saw Big Ed in front of his men and something like a scream left his parched lips. He started to run towards deliverance, forgetting the rope, which twanged tight with a humming jerk that yanked him off his feet. In the same moment Dick Webb involuntarily pulled the head of his horse around as he saw Fischer's men bearing down on him and the bewildered Billy Luskam, who was caught flatfooted in the middle of the street, rooted to the spot in panicked indecision.

Billy Luskam turned fast now and tried to make it to the safety of the porch of the store, but even as he made the decision, Fischer's men were on him with their guns blazing. He went down in the dirt, his body riddled by a dozen close range shots. The thundering phalanx of horsemen rolled right over his tattered corpse even as Dick Webb hauled his animal around. The beast was curvetting and twisting, startled by the rattling boom of the gunfire that the advancing riders were throwing at Webb.

Frank Angel reached the shelter of the saloon porch, emptying his own sixgun and the spare he had been carrying in a rolling fusillade of shots that took two Fischer men out of their saddles as if they had been swatted off with planks. Angel's shots turned the column sharply aside, the men yanking their horses around so that they were between the house in the open space between the saloon and the livery stable, piling out of the saddle to scurry to cover behind the stable's walls. Now Angel could hear Doc Day's big old Sharp's booming regularly from the roof of the jail and knew that the added firepower had momentarily saved Dick Webb's life. Reloading with fingers that fumbled from haste, he angled himself to the corner of the porch ready for a run to assist the kid, but even as he tensed ready, the Fischer men, hunkered down and steadied behind the livery stable, threw out a volley of shots. Dick Webb threw up a hand as if pointing the way to heaven, reeling in the saddle, trying to stay on the horse. Then his leg came out of the stirrup and he went over and down like a broken toy. He hit the ground with a heavy, hopeless thud. The panicked horse buck-jumped away from the inert figure and as it did, something – perhaps the burn of a too-close bullet, or simply the sudden renewed rattle of firearms – spooked it. The horse reared up high, forelegs coming down perilously close to the head of the fallen youngster, and then it lit out. Ears back, eyes rolling, it went straight across the street from standing start into full gallop. The rope attached to the pommel spanged taut and whipped Trev Rawley off his feet. He went up and came down flat behind the screeching horse, agony distorting his face into a terrible mask as his flailing fingers tried to loosen the noose on his neck.

'Kill that horse!' someone screamed, and Angel saw a

man run out from behind the livery stable, throw himself flat in the dirt of the street, levelling a Winchester on cradling elbows. He never fired it. From the roof of the jail, Doc Day's old Sharp's thundered, and the man flopped up and down, dead, while the panicked horse, only the whites of its eyes showing now, stampeded up the street, dragging the threshing, flailing, bumping thing that was Trev Rawley behind it. There was an awful silence for what seemed like long seconds, and then someone Angel did not know ran out into the street and tried to stop the animal, arms spreadeagled. The horse ran straight into the man, smashing him in a heap to the ground, then veered wide, the awful tattered thing behind it skidding around in the burning dust slamming against the verticals of the board-walk with a dull heavy sound that carried clearly the length of the street. Then the horse was past the livery stable, a hail of shots driving it off the street with the bumping, bloody, ragged, obscene thing behind it.

For a brief moment the men behind the livery stable watched the spot where the horse had disappeared between two houses in silent awe. Angel realised that this was about the only chance he was going to get and without stopping to think about it, ran out into the middle of the street where Dick Webb lay. As he reached the kid, a great shout went up from Fischer's men and they laid down a hasty volley of shots. One ran out into the street to get a better aim and Doc Day whanged him off his feet with a bullet from the Sharp's as Angel hoisted the groaning youngster on his shoulder and ran like a deer for the doorway of the jail. Bullets zipped past, chunked into the adobe, smacked whirring splinters from the wooden shutters as Doc Day fell down the ladderway inside the jail, throwing open the door through which Angel stumbled, half falling, his breath gone as he heaved Dick Webb inside and fell in after him. Doc flung the heavy door shut and slammed the solid crossbar into place as great hammering sounds signalled that the Fischer riders were venting their frustration on the door and walls. Slices of wood burst half-out of the heavy oak, but none of the bullets actually penetrated it. Angel pushed Doc Day aside, vaulting up the ladderway and on to the roof, throwing himself prone behind the foot-high parapet. Two men were running flat out across the street towards the jail, their rifles cocked upwards in their hands, attention fixed on the doorway beneath Angel.

'Steady, now,' Angel said to himself.

Then he shot them both as calmly as if he had been practising in the echoing Armoury situated in the basement of the Justice Department building, watched by the old Quartermaster-Sergeant who took care of the guns. The first man went sideways into the dust, his legs kicking high in agony. The second one stopped abruptly, an astonished look on his face. There was a bright red spot between his squinting eyes and he was dead long before he fell beside his companion, burying his face in the hock-deep dust.

Once again there was a momentary silence, then a yell of rage followed by a chattering volley of shots that hammered hunks out of the adobe walls, chipping flickering fragments of stone off the edges of the parapet as Angel, keeping his head down, wormed back towards the trapdoor and called down to Doc Day below.

'How is he, Doc?'

Day was bending over Dick Webb, who lay on the floor where Angel had dropped him. The boy's chest was dark with blood where Day had ripped away his shirt. The doctor grunted an unintelligible reply to Angel's question, his mind fully occupied with tending the boy's wound. Once more Angel reloaded his guns, firing a few shots at random towards the livery stable, more to let the Fischer gang know that their shots had been ineffective, more an act of defiance than anything else.

'Doc?' he called again. 'How's the kid?'

'He could be better than this,' was Day's tight-lipped reply. Looking down, Angel could see that Dick Webb's eyes were open, glazed with pain.

'Frank?' Dick Webb said. 'You there?'

'Lie still,' Day told him. 'Frank's here.'

'Uh?'

'You've been hurt,' the doctor said. 'Just lie still.'

'I remember,' Dick said, weakly. 'I remember Rawley in the street.'

'Damn fool play,' Day grunted.

'What happened then?'

'Your timing was perfect,' Angel told him. 'You came in one end of town, and Ed Fischer came in the other exactly the same time. After that, things got – interesting.'

'Interesting!' snorted Doc Day.

Dick Webb tried to smile, but before he could get his face shaped right the smile slid off and he went over the edge of consciousness into a dead faint. Doc Day laid him down gently, rolling his jacket to make a pillow for the youngster's head. He looked up at Angel and nodded, and Angel gave him a thumbs-up sign. It was probably as well that the kid was out of it for the moment, anyway.

Now he checked his gunbelt, and then Dick Webb's, piling the cartridges in front of him. He saw the Doctor looking at him and raised his eyebrows, holding up a cartridge.

'Not too damned many,' Day told him. 'How about you.'

'Much the same,' Angel said. 'We get all our good news at once, don't we?' Surrounded, low on ammunition, outgunned and outnumbered, the kid wounded and no chance of help before sundown tomorrow at the earliest, their picture could hardly have been called rosy. Even the jail, although it was solid, wasn't impregnable.

Ah, well, he thought. He wondered what had happened to Trev Rawley.

CHAPTER TEN

Trev Rawley wasn't dead, but he was damned near it.

He lay now on a pile of straw in the livery stable, where Ed Fischer's men had brought him. The panicked horse had tangled itself in some scrub behind the house across the street; Dick Boyd had sent a couple of men over there while there was a lull in the firing. They had carried the bleeding hulk down along the arroyo beneath the bridge at the south end of town and up behind the houses to the stable.

Big Ed looked down at the mess of Rawley's face and body and he shuddered. Raw, pulped, a mass of torn flesh with great skinless patches that looked like peeled tomato, the marshal's whole frame was an obscene mess of black and yellow and purple and bloody red, the clothing hanging in tattered strips, stuck to the dozens of deep gashes and ragged cuts which oozed blood on to the heedless straw. His hair was matted and thick with dried blood, his throat an awful raw thing totally stripped of skin by the searing rope. Rawley's voice was totally gone: he could not speak, nor cry out in search of relief from the scouring, burning agony which was devouring him. Twisting, whimpering, he rolled and bucked on the makeshift palliasse, lost in some mad red world of pain.

'God damn you!' Big Ed said to the thing on the ground.

Dick Boyd heard the words, and came over to stand beside Fischer.

'Take it easy, Ed,' he said, softly. 'He's bad hurt.'

'Good,' snapped Fischer savagely. 'If it hadn't been for him we wouldn't be bayed up here like some wagon-train full of pilgrims in Comanche country! If it hadn't been for him being led like some kind of stinking circus animal in front of the whole rotten town, we'd have just rode in and taken Mister Angel – like that!' He snapped his fingers to show how easy it would have been. 'Instead of which, the bastard is forted up in the strongest building in town, it's damned near nightfall, and it'll take . . . ' His voice trailed off and he looked thoughtful.

'Who the hell is in there, anyway?' he said softly.

'Dunno,' Boyd told him. 'But whoever it is, they can shoot. By the sound of the gun, it's Doc Day. Angel and the kid, of course, we know are in there. Mebbe others: I dunno. But those bastards can shoot, Ed. We've lost half our men, and I've got three others wounded.'

'You see,' Fischer said, kicking the ruined sole of the marshal's boot. 'You see?'

Trev Rawley rolled his head from side to side, his eyes staring and wide, clouded with immense pain. If he knew what Ed had said, there was no sign of it.

'All right,' Fischer said. 'Get a couple of men over to the store. See if there's any blasting powder in there. If there is, bring everything you can carry down here!'

'Blasting p—?' Dick Boyd's mouth fell open. 'But Ed – you aiming to blast them out? What about Joe? The whole place will go up! You can't—'

'*Can't?*' roared Ed Fischer. '*Can't?*'

He caught the man in a vice-like grip, smashing Boyd back against the wooden wall of the stable, shaking the door-frame. Boyd's breath whistled out of his body, and he shook his head in panic.

'You – tell – me – I – can't?' snarled Ed Fischer.

'No, Ed – no,' Boyd managed. 'No!'

'I can do anything I want to do!' Fischer told him, releasing his hold. Boyd slumped back, eyes wide with fear. 'My stupid brother got himself in this mess. Expects me to get him out the same way I always have. Well, the hell with him! This time I look after Number One! Number One!' Fischer shouted, smacking his fist against his chest. If he noticed the astonished looks of his remaining riders, he did not show it.

'Well?' he roared at Boyd. 'Get at it, damn you!'

For a moment, Dick Boyd just stared at his leader, and then he broke and ran, tapping two of his men on the shoulder and running crouched from the back of the stable across the alley to the rear of the saloon and again to the store next door to it.

Twenty minutes later they were back. They had blasting powder in cans, coal-oil, caps, everything they needed.

'Now,' Fischer gloated, looking out of the shattered window towards the looming hulk of the jail, a solid dark blur in the shadowed darkness of the street outside. 'Now, you stinking rats! Let's see how you like these apples!'

Apart from a few sporadic shots from across the street, it had been quiet since nightfall. Doc had boiled up some pretty revolting coffee on the big potbellied stove while they took stock of their situation. They fed some of the bitter hot brew to the kid, who was sitting up, albeit wincing every time he moved his wounded shoulder.

Angel confessed himself somewhat puzzled by the fact that Fischer and his men had not long since tried to rush the jail. They had everything going for them: superior weight, more firepower. It didn't figure, unless Fischer's crew had been more badly hurt than he thought. He tried to recall how many men he'd seen in the rushing moments when the column had thundered down the street. Ten, twelve? It was hard to say. He looked at Doc's powder-grimed face, the wrinkles at the corners of the medico's eyes looking as if they had been painted on white. Dick was alert now, and if worst came to worst, could probably handle a pistol with his left hand.

'I sure as hell could use a skillet of bacon and eggs,' the kid said, with a wry grin. 'How about you?'

'Sure,' Angel said.

'Maybe we could just step up the street to the Chinaman's and get us some,' Doc suggested.

'Love to,' Dick Webb said, playing the tired joke along. 'But right now business is a little confining.'

They fell silent for a moment, then Dick Webb spoke.

'Frank,' he said. 'You think we've got any chance at all?'

Angel shrugged.

'Hard to tell,' he said. 'If your sister can make it through to Fort Union, or even Springer, we can pull through.'

'Hell, don't try that on me,' Dick Webb said. 'That's a good two days' riding.'

'Don't spit on your luck,' Angel said. 'They might run into a patrol.'

'And pigs might fly,' the doctor said. 'What the hell are those guys shooting at now?'

The cause for this question was another heavy outburst of firing directed against the front of the jail. The guns boomed and boomed again across the street, flashes of lancing flame streaking out from the windows and doorways of the livery stable. They heard the flat whack of lead smashing into the adobe, and Angel turned towards the doctor with a quizzical look, his eyebrows raised.

It was at that moment that the explosion happened.

The jail was built in the shape of a thick 'L' with its lower arm fronting the street. In the upright, the two big cells were paralleled by a corridor which had a door at its far end, behind the building, through which the prisoners were taken to the latrines. Another door halfway along this corridor led into the big room in which Angel and his friends were sitting and it burst open with a tremendous crash, tearing off its hinges and smashing into the corner of the room as the enormous explosion ripped half of the wall behind the jail apart with a thunderous roar.

With a shouted warning to Doc Day, Angel's hands flashed for his guns as three men loomed dark and huge in the doorway, misted in swirling dust and fumes, their guns blasting wildly through into the room. Angel threw himself to one side and his own guns blazed four times as he rolled across the floor. Two of the dark shapes folded to the floor in front of him. Behind him he thought he saw Dick Webb thumbing a fast shot into the murk, but he had no time to look longer. He moved out fast into the hallway, stumbling over fallen brick, guns up and ready as he saw a man running towards the back of the jail across the open ground outside. He saw the man's gun come up and fired in the same instant that the running man did. A streak of red hot pain touched Angel's body beneath his right arm and he spun off to the left, smacking against the wall of the cells, half falling in the jumbled darkness. The man outside cart-wheeled over and down and Angel didn't see him any more.

Then there was a moment of complete silence, as if God had ordained a moment for the living to identify the dead. Angel turned around and there behind him was Joe Fischer, stepping over the fallen door of his cell, the gun he had picked up from one of the attackers in his hand, and the feral light of murder in his eyes.

'Angel?' he said.

Doc shot him from about three feet away with the Sharp's and Angel would remember the awful meaty smack of the bullet hitting Joe Fischer's body for many and many a long nightmare. Joe's whole body was smashed against the adobe cell wall as if some mighty hand had swatted him like a fly, and he slid down into the rubble, leaving a ghastly smear streaking the wall.

Day stepped into the broken corridor, his eyes glaring through a mask of adobe dust. There was blood on his shirt, and Angel put out a hand to touch it, but Doc smiled and waved him away.

'It's from Dick's shoulder,' he said. 'I'm all right.'

His reassuring tone suddenly altered, his eyes widening as he looked over Angel's shoulder.

'Fire!' he shouted. 'They've set the place afire!'

CHAPTER ELEVEN

'Hell's teeth!' shouted Angel.

He ran into the jumbled room where Dick Webb lay sprawled, the sixgun still ready in his left hand. The boy's face was white with pain and his eyes looked slightly fey, as though his thoughts were not altogether there. He needed better attention than the doctor could give him in this mess, Angel thought. But there was no time for that now. He grabbed the water bucket and ran towards the back of the building, hurling the water at the place where he could see the first reaching yellow tongues of flame seeking an entrance between the curling, blackening floorboards. The sound of them was a steady, whirring roar, and over the stink of smoke was a resiny, sharp tang that told Angel the fire had been started with coal oil. The water forced the flames into retreat for a moment, and then he saw Doc come stumbling across the broken brick, over the fallen bodies of their attackers, another water bucket in his hands slopping over. Angel took it from him and hurled it into the centre of the once-more vigorous flames. Again there was the hiss of defeat, the clouds of steam from the frustrated fire, but now there was no more water, and nothing with which to fight the flames but an old sack. Angel beat at the surging flame with the smouldering sack, sparks flickering up along the doorjambs, flames following them around him as he worked, coughing, retching, hearing the slight fizz of his own hair singeing, driven back remorselessly by the increasing heat. His clothes were scorching now and he could no longer get near the dancing, wicked spread of flame that was advancing eagerly into the narrow corridor fanned by the draught of wind that came through the broken walls and doorway. Small pieces of charred wood and ash floated in the heavy, hot air. It would only be minutes before the entire jail was an inferno from which nothing could escape. Angel fell back from the rolling black smoke, his eyes gummed with dried tears that never formed in the immense heat.

'Can't stop it!' he shouted, falling back near Day and the kid. They looked at each other, but said nothing. Dick Webb got to his feet slowly, painfully, hitching at his belt with one hand.

'That's all, then,' he said, to no one in particular, cocking the gun in his left hand. There was another, stronger, sweeter smell now, and they gagged on it. The bodies sprawled in the shattered corridor were beginning to burn.

Angel touched Day's shoulder and gestured with his chin towards the heavy bar on the door. There was no place left to go but out through there, out towards the waiting guns of the Fischer riders. Dead if they stayed, dead if they didn't. He looked at Dick Webb. The kid's face was grim: he wanted to go out fighting. Angel's brain raced furiously. He had to find some way to stop the kid rushing out with a gun in his hand to certain, sudden death.

'Angel!'

He heard the voice through the angry roar of the flames and knew it was Big Ed Fischer.

'I hear you!' he yelled back.

'You're finished, Angel!' screamed Fischer. 'Come on out while you can – or burn, damned if I care which!'

'We're out of chips, kid,' Angel said softly.

Dick Webb looked at him, his face surprised, contempt creeping into his eyes. The kid looked at Doc, who was watching Angel with a look of puzzlement.

'We can make a run for it, Frank!' Doc coughed. As he spoke, one of the heavy roof beams crashed to the floor at the far end of the corridor. A long spiralling shower of sparks climbed up into the star-studded velvet of the sky.

'We've got maybe a minute,' Angel said, tightly. He raised his voice to a shout. 'All right, Fischer!' he shouted. 'We're coming out!'

There was a ragged shout of triumph outside, then they

heard Ed Fischer's voice again. 'Throw out your guns!' he shouted.

Angel nodded to the other two, tossing his own sixgun out as he unbarred the door and swung it open. After a moment, with a look of utter contempt plain now on his face in the bright redness of the flames, Dick Webb followed suit. Angel nodded to Day, who threw his Sharp's away from him as if he suddenly detested it.

Frank Angel swung wide the heavy door and stumbled out into the street, followed by the other two. The whole area was bathed in a terrible bright red light from the burning jail behind him, and with the added draught caused by the opening of the door, the flames surged higher and higher, as if rejoicing in their victory. Coughing, retching, eyes streaming from the smoke, the three men came out into the street where Ed Fischer stood triumphant, a Winchester repeater cradled in his hamlike hands, alone in the middle of the glaring dusty street.

'Get out here where I can see you!' he yelled. 'I'm going to enjoy this!'

Behind the three men there was a roaring rumbling crash as the roof of the jail finally collapsed, great lumps of flaming wood and ash floating high like giant fireflies in the night sky, huge spirals of glowing sparks wending upwards into infinity. They could see now that a ring of townspeople, their faces strained in the flickering red light, were standing watching the awful dénouement of their resistance. Fischer seemed oblivious of everything: the fire, the people, everything except the three men who stood now helpless in front of him, their clothes smouldering with tiny burns, faces grimed from the billowing smoke.

'Get over here!' he yelled, gesturing abruptly with the Winchester. 'I want everyone in this stinking town to see you!'

'You better let us move away from here, Fischer,' Angel said. 'Or we'll fry in this heat!' He moved forward a few tentative steps.

'You'll fry all right,' Fischer gloated. 'But in Hell!'

He gestured again with the rifle: *move* ! and Angel made a cautious half circle around to the side, his eyes on the ground as if afraid to stumble.

'Now they're going to see something!' Fischer crowed, gloating triumph in his voice. 'Now I'll hang you and they'll watch, and they'll remember who hanged you and why. They'll all think twice before they ever challenge a Fischer again! It's still my town, Angel! Still my town!'

His head was thrown back towards the sky as he shouted the last words, glorying in them like some victorious, insane animal.

'You don't have to hang us, do you?' Angel croaked, and Doc Day's head came up sharply as he heard the tone in Angel's voice. He could have sworn there was fear in it. He shook his head, not believing, but Angel's next words confirmed it.

'Please,' Angel begged. 'Just let us ride out of here. We won't give you any trouble. We'll—'

'Listen to him!' screeched Ed Fischer, waving a hand at the people who still stood, stock-still, watching. 'Listen to him! Get over here, all of you! I want you to see him crawling, begging for his life!'

Nobody moved.

'Get over here!' Fischer shouted again, turning his head towards the unmoving spectators. '*Get over here*!'

And in the moment that he turned his head, Frank Angel moved.

CHAPTER TWELVE

Angel had worked it out, figured the odds.

In this one incredibly fast movement he put everything he had on the line, using every ounce of the strength and skill he had acquired during his long months of training with the Department of Justice, every iota of himself summoned in this half second, to this place, his body a machine to do the bidding of his racing brain.

His right arm shot sideways, jarring Dick Webb off his feet with a shout of pain, knocking the boy down to the ground. Fischer whirled around, the Winchester bearing down on the source of the sound and giving Angel the fraction of a second he had gambled for. The Winchester takes just that millisecond longer to move, to use, than a sixgun and in it Angel had dropped left and rolled, his own right hand finding the sixgun close to which he had so carefully placed himself, the same sixgun that Dick Webb had earlier tossed contemptuously into the dusty street.

Fischer was very fast, his reactions galvanised by the adrenalin already pumping through him, and he lined up desperately on the rolling figure of Frank Angel. He was very good, not an easy man to take; but he had been that half second behind Angel all the way and that made him a dead man. Angel's shot smashed upwards into the open, snarling mouth and drove straight through, bursting Fischer's skull and splattering the man's brain outwards in a ghastly misting spray of pinkish-grey. The Winchester exploded in the reflexive jerking of the dead man's finger, but the bullet drove harmlessly into the earth two yards from Angel, who was now up on one knee, sighting – as Dick Boyd reacted to the sudden movement, eyes wildly seeking a target as his men scattered for some kind of shelter, snatching at their guns as Boyd went down flat dead with Angel's second bullet in his heart, the drawn sixshooter sliding from his nerveless fingers into the dirt beside him.

Now Doc was running flat out for the store across the street, flinching as bullets zipped around him, dodging like a deer while Angel emptied his sixgun towards the hidden Fischer riders hunkered down behind a water trough in front of the house down the street from the smouldering, flickering ruins of the destroyed jail. Angel's fire put them out of action long enough for Dick Webb to squirrel back for shelter around the side of the ruined, charred but still-solid wall of the old jail.

'For God's sake!' he shouted as one of the townspeople ran past him to safety, 'give me a gun! Somebody give me a gun!'

Even as he yelled the words, he saw Angel's body flinch hard and to the right, his head jerking around fast as a bullet touched him, and then Doc Day cut loose from the porch of the saloon with a shotgun, the shotgun Billy Luskam had dropped when he ran out into the street and was killed. The huge *baroomph*! dulled the shouts of running people and Webb saw one of the Fischer men leap upwards and out like some strange fish rising to bait, falling across the water trough and hanging there, body shattered, arms dangling. The remaining three men there laid a heavy fire across the street and Doc ducked back to shelter, reloading.

Angel was down on one knee in the middle of the street now, supporting himself with one hand, pawing with the other at the blood which trickled down into his eyes from the ragged cut across his temple just below the hairline. His eyes were unfocused from the smashing impact of the near-miss.

'Somebody give me a gun!' Dick Webb yelled again, but there was no one even near him now, and the street was empty except for the macabre figure of the reeling Angel, trying to get to his feet.

'Get down, Frank!' Dick yelled at the top of his voice. '*Down, down, down*!' He gritted his teeth as he waited for the shot to come from behind the water trough, but there was silence and he could not understand why. Turning his head, he saw the reason.

Swaying there, his hand on the hitchrail, was the most awful sight Dick Webb had ever seen. Almost naked, his body so torn and bloody and broken that it did not seem possible he could even stand, a sixgun dangling from his nerveless, stripped fingers, stood Trev Rawley.

'Agghhhhl' he shouted. His voice was like the last call for help at the end of the world, inhuman, eerie.

Frank Angel heard the sound, and seemed to know that it was his name that the sound was supposed to be. He turned towards the place it had come from, the empty sixgun still in his hand.

'Anngghhhhl,' said the thing.

Angel stumbled towards the sound. He shook his head, trying to clear it of the red mist before his eyes, the awful resonant pounding roar in his brain. 'Rawley?' he said, his voice puzzled. 'Rawley?'

The people bayed in safe places along the street watched in hushed awe.

Dick Webb got slowly to his feet. His shoulder hurt like hell.

It didn't seem possible that Rawley could walk across to where Frank Angel was, but he was doing it, doing it when everything in nature screamed that it was not possible for anyone so badly hurt to even try. Tatterdemalion, a spastic, twitching bloody wreck, he lurched forward, putting one foot in front of the other once, twice, then hesitantly again. Dead on his feet, he moved inexorably, relentlessly, raw nerve ends twitching visibly in the pulped face, mad empty eyes glaring with only one desire, the desire that kept him moving – to kill the man in front of him. Two steps more and then two more he made, and still no one moved.

Angel stood there waiting, his head canted to one side, trying to place exactly where the threat was coming from. He heard the sibilant hiss of the footfall in the soft dust. But where, *where*?

'Yougghh,' Trev Rawley said, in that ghastly whisper. 'Youggggghh.'

It was as he spoke the second time that the bright red mist in front of Angel's eyes cleared slightly and he saw clearly. Rawley – this awful thing was Trev Rawley! – was only three yards away, the sixgun still at his side, and everyone watching, transfixed by the spectacle they could see and yet still not believe.

'Youggghh. D . . . Zzassssth.' *You did this*, he was saying.

Angel shook his head, and the movement dizzied him. He went down on one knee, hearing a sharp intake of breath from the people watching nearby. Why were they standing watching? Why didn't they help? Damn them all!

'Bggggg,' Rawley said. *Beg.*

He lifted the sixgun very slowly, lining the yawning barrel up not more than a foot from Angel's head. The barrel wavered, trembled as the awful apparition in front of Angel used every atom of its will to do the bidding of the crazed mind. The skinless thumb curled over the spurred hammer, slowly forcing it back.

Angel's hand moved.

Up and outward it moved, away from the side of his boot in an underhand throwing movement, releasing the flat-bladed, razor-edged knife which Angel had slid from its hiding place. Long, long before this moment he had spent arguing hours with the Armourer in the echoing basement of the Justice Building figuring ways in which a man might carry, undetected, weapons which would not be discovered in the normal, cursory search. One of their ideas had been twin knives, of finest Solingen steel, each perfectly balanced for throwing. It was the right-hand one of these which Angel had plucked from its scabbard between the inner and outer lining of his boot. It sped like a streak of molten silver across the space between the two men and buried itself to the haft in Trev Rawley's throat.

The man spun around, eyes bulging as he tried to scream over the awful slicing rigidity inside him, the pistol dropping from his hand as his fingers plucked themselves to bloody ribbons on the wicked blade. He opened his mouth and a horrid gout of thick black blood burst from it, joining the pumping wetness beneath his chin.

His sightless eyes fixed themselves on some distant place and turned inwards upon themselves. Then he fell in a long straight line, going down like some lightning-shattered pine, flattening out and emptying curiously, like a slightly deflated balloon.

Angel looked up, helpless now if Fischer's men used their guns on him. But no shots came.

He thought he could see Doc Day over by the water-trough, his shotgun menacing the men behind it. He thought he could see townspeople running to help Dick Webb. He stood swaying for a moment as people ran to help him and he nodded, as if this confirmed something he had been thinking.

Then he slid softly sideways into the dust, face down in the blood of the last of Ed Fischer's killers.

CHAPTER THIRTEEN

There is a place you go when you are very badly hurt, or very very tired, everything gone past some undefinable point of no return. It is a strangely comforting place, not quite as far away from life as death itself, but well beyond the borders of mere unconsciousness. You float there, weightless, formless, moving with effortless ease across mighty boundaries of time. Sometimes the strong elasticity of life pulls you towards the shallows of this blackness, near enough to hear voices, sounds, movements around you. None of them means anything.

In the darkness where you are, all sorts of wondrous things are possible. Angel was there now, remembering things he did not even know he knew and would forget again, living a dozen lives in places which never existed. It was a slow-moving, mysterious place he explored, tempted always to go ever deeper into the blackest dark by siren calls which made no sound.

He stayed in this soft world, safe, warm, caressed sensuously by tangible dreams spoiled only when true memory spilled like water across the nerve-ends of his mind. Once he remembered fire. It was a bad memory and he recoiled from it, going back down to the warm softness in the dark below memory. Then another memory: a staring, awful face, skinless, its mad eyes staring into the windows of his mind. He felt pain for the first time, a dull, solid throbbing in the side of his head. He came back from where he had been and opened his eyes.

'He's awake,' he heard someone say.

A face floated into his range of vision: a pretty girl he had never seen before, her eyes dark and concerned, her long black hair falling forward to brush his cheek as she bent over him. She looked familiar, as though he should know her.

'You're pretty,' he told her.

He closed his eyes on the picture of her fixed in his mind, intending to take it back with him down into the warm darkness and centre endless dreams around it, but the drumming in his head persisted, and now he could feel the surge of life inside himself and he could not go back any more. Once you hear the sound of life, you can no longer find the frontiers of the other place.

He opened his eyes again, a moment later to him. It was almost a full twenty-four hours since the last time he had awakened. The girl was gone, but there was someone sitting by his bed. He turned his head and saw a face he recognised.

'Dick?' he said, 'is that you?'

The boy nodded, and Angel frowned to see that he was crying. That seemed a strange thing to do, and he said so.

'Sure, Frank,' the boy said, smiling at last. 'Sure it's plain dumb.' He patted Angel on the forearm as the man in the bed closed his eyes smiling, just relaxing now, not even sleeping. Coming through. Dick Webb watched him. There was no way he could tell him yet that he had been on the edge of death for four days, Doc Day swearing over his lack of response, his own failure to do much more than stand by and hope that Nature would mend Angel's concussed brain. No, he'd tell him all that later.

He'd tell him about Doc Day, and how the townspeople had finally rallied around him to frogmarch the remaining Fischer riders across the street to lock them into the dank confines of the cellar of the Silver King. He'd tell Angel how Doc had singlehandedly stopped the crowd from hanging the gibbering Regenvogel, whom they'd dragged from his house down the street, and how Susie and Deluvina had reached Fort Union. How they had found a young Lieutenant there named Evans who reacted to Angel's name as if it had been that of General Phil Sheridan himself. With an Army patrol Evans had ridden at forced-march speeds all the way up to the Crossing, but far too late to do much more than mop up and take the sullen remnants of Big Ed Fischer's fighting men down to Fort Union for trial. Young Lieutenant Evans took charge of the town, declaring martial law, organising burial parties, gangs of men to clear the wreckage of the old jail and start work upon another. By the time Angel regained consciousness, Fischer's Crossing was back to some kind of normal life.

He'd tell him all that. He'd tell him too, at the right time, that the young Lieutenant wanted to see him, and that he had a message for him from Washington. But there was plenty of time for all that: it would keep until Angel was on his feet again.

'How are you feeling?' he asked.

'Damned hungry,' Angel told him, smiling.

'We can soon fix that,' Dick Webb said.

And they damned soon did.

CHAPTER FOURTEEN

She was a tall young woman with honey-blonde hair usually tied back with a ribbon. Today it swung loose across her shoulders. Today was different. Today she had left home knowing that Frank Angel was back and that he would be in to report to the Attorney-General and although she was a little bit annoyed with herself for making this concession to her own femininity, this admission that she wanted Frank Angel to notice her, admire her, she wasn't so annoyed that she didn't enjoy knowing it had made him do just that, or enjoy knowing that Angel was watching her walk and admiring that, too. So her eyes were impish, her chin lifted a fraction above normal, and if she swung her hips a fraction more than you might have expected the personal private secretary of the Attorney-General of the United States to do, well, Amabel Rowe wasn't at all sure that being the Attorney-General's secretary was necessarily the most interesting thing a woman might do with her life.

So she preceded Frank Angel down the corridor of the big old building on Pennsylvania Avenue which was the headquarters of the Department of Justice, towards the first floor office of the Attorney-General with its leather-studded doors flanked by two Marines.

Angel followed her with a slight smile on his lips. Amabel was a very beautiful girl, and he'd thought so for a long time. Which was why, not ten minutes earlier, he had asked her to have dinner with him that evening in a nice little restaurant he knew over in Georgetown. Amabel wasn't the kind of woman to play coy. She'd said yes straight off, a little light of promise dancing in her eyes. A man couldn't ask to see more than that in any woman's eyes.

She stopped now in the antechamber outside the Attorney-General's office. The two Marines stiffly at attention outside the leather-studded doors affected not to notice either of them. Angel could see their eyes move as

Amabel crossed towards her desk. He pitied the two soldiers: the thought of having to stand mute and silent, no more noticeable than a candlestick, while someone like Amabel walked around in front of you all day was something he could not imagine doing. But then, he reflected, uniforms do something to some people: about what a prefrontal lobotomy does for others. He stood waiting while Amabel went into the Attorney-General's office, heard the growl of The Man as she told him who was waiting. Then she came out of the doorway and beckoned him, and Angel went forward, passing her as she came out.

'Seven o'clock,' he whispered.

She said nothing but a flush rose up from beneath the high neck of her dress, touching her cheeks with peach-bloom pink, and she went across to her desk struggling not to let the laughter escape her lips. Angel realised why: just behind the half-open door the Attorney-General was standing glowering at him. Had he heard?

'Come in, come in,' he was told. He glanced back at the girl, who was busily writing something, her head down. She looked up as the Attorney-General started to close the door.

'Now, young man,' she heard her boss say in his best 'My-God-have-I-got-to-do-everything' voice. 'Just where the hell do you think you've been? And what's all this about Fischer's—'

The rest was cut off by the closing of the door, but she could envisage the two of them quite clearly and what they would be saying to each other. The Attorney-General would be opening his humidor and lighting one of his awful cigars, sitting back in the big chair by the tall window, waiting for Angel's report.

'Well, sir,' Angel would be saying, 'it's kind of a long story.'

'That's all right,' the Attorney-General would reply. 'Take as long as you like. Take all night if you need to.'

Amabel Rowe let the smile come into full blossom now.

He'd better not.